Just One Date

THE BILLIONAIRE BARONS OF TEXAS ∽ BOOK ONE

CHRIS KENISTON

Indie House Publishing

Indie House Publishing

MORE BOOKS

By Chris Keniston

The Billionaire Barons of Texas

Just One Date
Just One Spark
Just One Dance
Just One Take
Just One Taste
Just One Shot
Just One Chance

Hart Land

Heather
Lily
Violet
Iris
Hyacinth
Rose
Calytrix
Zinnia
Poppy
Picture Perfect

Farraday Country

Adam
Brooks
Connor
Declan
Ethan
Finn
Grace

Hannah
Ian
Jamison
Keeping Eileen
Loving Chloe
Morgan
Neil

Honeymoon Series
Honeymoon for One
Honeymoon for Three
Honeymoon for Four
Honeymoon for Five

Aloha Romance Series:
Aloha Texas
Almost Paradise
Mai Tai Marriage
Dive Into You
Look of Love
Love by Design
Love Walks In
Shell Game
Flirting with Paradise

Surf's Up Flirts:
(Aloha Series Companions)
Shall We Dance
Love on Tap
Head Over Heels
Perfect Match
Just One Kiss
It Had to Be You
Cat's Meow

CHAPTER ONE

"**O**ur grandfather, a man richer than Bezos, offered to pay for the wedding, and the future Mrs. Andrew Mason told him no?" Chase James Baron, head of Baron Enterprises and confirmed bachelor, tipped his brandy snifter at his sister Eve. "The more I learn about Nancy, the more I like her."

As far as their grandfather, a former Marine turned politician, was currently concerned, each of his grandchildren should have six children – just as he and his wife of sixty years had done. Andrew's mother, Amanda Baron Mason, was the youngest and closest in age to Chase's father, Bradley Baron. Bradley had garnered his father's approval by marrying young, and well, although he only had five children, instead of the expected six. Unfortunately for Bradley, divorcing Chase's mother and working his way through three more wives had not gone over nearly as well with the proud former governor. Even if the unions had added two more grandchildren to the fold.

Now their grandfather was clearly tiring of waiting for his grandchildren to continue the tradition of having a large family. So far, much to former Governor James Earnest Baron's chagrin, every last one of his progeny was woefully behind the curve in finding a spouse and increasing the troops – his loving reference to his family. Except for Andrew, who had been caught and reeled in by his new bride-to-be.

Andrew and Nancy's nuptials had brought Chase to Galveston in preparation of the first, long-awaited, wedding of his generation. He and his siblings, Craig, Mitch and Eve were waiting for their brother Kyle onboard his yacht—a favorite family gathering spot—to leave for a quiet sail along the Gulf coast before the upcoming festivities, and ensuing chaos began.

"You're going to love Nancy," his sister Eve said with a smile. "Smart and sassy. Perfect for Andrew. Even though the Governor grumbles about her stubbornness—often—I think he really likes her."

"If it means finally having a great-grandchild, I think he'd let Lucrezia Borgia into the fold." Chase would have laughed at his own joke if he didn't think it held a grain of truth. "At least Andrew and Nancy will take the pressure off the rest of us grandchildren to breed."

Eve almost snorted her brandy. "What planet are you living on? If anything it's made the Governor more determined to increase the family troops. Oh, wait. That's right. You hide out in your Dallas man cave. Sleep, eat, and breathe Baron Enterprises. I must say, moving the operations to the downtown high rise, including a penthouse apartment, made for an affordable commute. You never even have to leave the building. Ever."

"Now you sound like the old man." Ten years ago when Chase had first come up with the mixed-use plans for the new headquarters, his grandfather had been delighted with the idea. Chase and his cousin Devlin, founder of one of the largest commercial real estate firms in the country, had worked out every detail before presenting it to their grandfather. That had been long before the patriarch had become obsessed with seeing his grandchildren procreate.

"*Never gonna meet a good woman if you live behind that desk. Balance, boy. Balance,*" Chase mimicked his grandfather.

"*You can take the man out of the military, but you can't take the military out of the man. Push, push, push.*" Eve tipped her head back and blew out a sigh. "Did you hear what he did to Craig?"

"At Mitch's fund-raiser last month?"

Eve nodded. "Craig made the mistake of telling the Governor that he was going stag to our dear brother the senator's event."

"Craig runs a major production company. Surely an up-and-coming actress would have been more than happy to have her photos splattered across every media outlet under the sun at a ten-thousand-dollar-a-plate dinner for the senate's golden boy."

"I don't think any of us realized the Governor has upped the ante. If we can't find our own dates, he'll find someone for us."

"And that is exactly why I am bringing my own date." Chase pushed to his feet and crossed the lounge of his brother's yacht to refill his drink. One of the stuffiest families on the social registry, the Van Kleins had married off all their children but one. And from his limited interactions with Gwyneth, her spinsterhood was for good reason. "I can't help but wonder, what was the Governor thinking, sticking Craig all night with Gwyneth Van Klein?"

Eve raised a single brow at her eldest brother, then shook her head. "The usual. Good stock. Wide hips. I swear, in this day and age, the old man still thinks of women as brood mares. He probably has Gwyneth's dental records."

"I'd be more worried that he probably has yours." Kyle, the missing sibling, came through the doorway. "Sorry I'm late. My meeting ran long. I see you've already helped yourself to refreshments."

"We skipped the lemonade and went straight for the

hard stuff." Eve smiled up at him.

"My Napoleon brandy." Kyle laughed. "Rough week?"

"The Governor gave me a lecture on my biological clock yesterday. And the day before—"

"And this morning," Kyle added, his eyes filled with sympathy. "Sorry, sis."

"I'm used to it. It's not like I don't want to meet a nice guy, but it's not easy when your last name is Baron."

Unfortunately, Chase knew exactly what she meant. Having a family fortune prominently reported for all to see, the Baron name was a golden ticket for swindlers and fortune hunters. He'd been there, done that, even bought the wardrobe. Which is why he'd decided, before ever setting foot near Galveston for his cousin's wedding, to preempt the former Governor's unwanted efforts to find his offspring suitable mates. Chase might not run a major film production company, but he'd seen *Pretty Woman*. While he wasn't stupid enough to hire a hooker to appease his grandfather's matchmaking attempts, Chase wasn't beyond hiring a good actress to redirect their grandfather's attention elsewhere.

The plan had merit. Strictly business. No emotions. No gold diggers. And best of all, no complications.

"You're getting paid to spend the next seven days with a man?" C. J. Lawson's head was ready to explode from her sister's latest crazy plan.

"Yes and no." Bev shrugged.

C.J. glared at her younger sister the same way she'd stare down a raw recruit and then drew upon years of military discipline not to scream in Bev's face. "You do realize those answers do not go together."

"Yes, for five thousand dollars now and five thousand

at the end of the week, I'm being paid to spend one week with Chase Baron but no not "*with*" with him."

"Do you know where you're staying?"

"Galveston."

C.J. refrained from rolling her eyes at her Pollyanna-like sister. "In a hotel?"

Nibbling on her lower lip, Bev hesitated a few minutes. "Maybe. He might have mentioned a boat."

"Okay." Who would have thought dealing with boots fresh off the bus would be easier than shaking some sense into her starry-eyed sister? "Maybe in a hotel, or a boat, but definitely in separate rooms?"

"Oh." Bev stopped tossing clothes into her suitcase. "I didn't ask."

Oh, brother. Never before had C.J. wished so hard that Bev had gotten a few less beauty genes and just a teensy-weensy bit more of the brains in the family. At five foot five and 110 pounds, with a twenty-four inch waist, and blue eyes the shade of an azure crayon, Bev conjured images of Marilyn Monroe, Judy Holiday, and a long list of talented women who got more from sex appeal than smarts. "How could you not ask about sleeping arrangements?"

"Because, for ten thousand dollars, I don't really care if he puts me on the roof."

"Or in his bed?"

Sweater in hand, Bev froze and looked up at her sister. "That wasn't part of the negotiations."

All set to ask "What negotiations?" since her sister didn't seem to have any answers other than a 10K salary in a one-week time frame, and something about fooling an old man, C.J.'s mind suddenly registered that Bev held a sweater. "Why are you packing cold-weather clothes for Galveston?"

"Oh, well, that's what I was getting around to explaining."

That pixie twinkle in Bev's eye was never a good sign. As a kid it could have meant anything from teaching the unwilling cat how to swim, to homemade hair dye. Neither of which had produced stellar results. "Then explain. Again."

"Okay." Bev flipped her long blonde hair behind her shoulder and sucked in a deep breath. "Chase's cousin is getting married in eight days. It's a big family wedding. All the siblings and cousins and aunts and uncles will be there. Even his mom, who is practically a hermit somewhere in Europe, is crossing the pond for her favorite nephew's wedding."

C.J. bobbed her head, encouraging her sister to get to whatever part of this plan she hadn't already heard.

"So Chase has this grandfather."

"Yes," C.J. quipped a bit impatiently. "You've mentioned that before. He wants to see all his grandchildren married. I got that part."

"Well, the Governor—"

"Governor?"

"That's the grandfather. Former governor of Texas, though I think it was a lot of years ago, and before that he was a Marine."

"*Is*," C.J. said without thinking.

"Oh, yeah." Bev sighed and echoed with her sister, "*Once a Marine, always a Marine.*"

"Right." C.J. nodded again, sorry she'd derailed her sister's story.

"To avoid the grandfather harassing and annoying and prodding and matchmaking and creating family drama at his cousin's wedding, I've been hired to be his date. Like *Pretty Woman*."

"You do remember she was a hooker?"

"Julia Roberts?"

Lord, C.J. loved her sister. Really she did. But the girl

had tested C.J.'s patience from the day their parents had brought Bev home from the hospital. "Vivian—the character in the movie—Vivian was a hooker."

"Oh, yeah. Whatever. He offered me 10K to be his date." Bev stopped and, biting on her lower lip again, raised her gaze to the ceiling in thought. "Maybe it was *girlfriend*." Smiling, she bobbed her head. "That was it. His girlfriend for a week."

"*Girlfriend*." C.J. could hear the whine in her voice. She hated people who whined. "And you didn't ask about sleeping arrangements?" Why couldn't Bev be something normal, like a manicurist or receptionist? Why an actress? "Never mind. Can we get back to the clothes?"

"Oh. Right." Bev perked up. "This morning I got a call from my friend Gloria. You remember Gloria?"

C.J. nodded. She had no clue who the heck Gloria was, but C.J. had no intention of letting this conversation go down another rabbit hole.

"Gloria got a small part in John Cipro's new movie. It's a minor character, but they need a lot of extras because they're filming out in the middle of nowhere, and she got me on the list of extras! If they like me, I might even get to say something." Bev practically jumped in place with glee.

"At least that's a legitimate gig. When does filming start?"

"Monday."

"This Monday?" Now C.J. was really confused.

"Yes. In Canada, where it's cold."

At least that explained the sweater. "So, why are we having this conversation, if you're not taking the job in Galveston?"

"Because you are."

CHAPTER TWO

"**A**re you seriously bringing an actress to a Baron family dinner?"

Hefting a casual shoulder, Chase turned to his sister. "Who better?"

"Oh, I don't know. Maybe, say, a date. A real one." Eve tossed her eldest brother a pointed glare.

"That's exactly what this is. Just one date with no strings or complications."

Pouring himself a drink, Kyle merely shook his head at Chase. "You won't fool our grandfather, and, even if he does think you're dating, that only shifts the focus from dating to marriage and babies."

"Maybe, but more likely"—Chase lifted his glass to examine the smooth honey-colored liquid within—"it will shift his focus to any one of his other single grandkids. Either way, it's a risk I'm willing to take."

"I'm only sorry I didn't think of it myself." Craig raised his glass to Chase. "Certainly would have saved me that insufferable night escorting Gwyneth."

"Come on, guys." Eve frowned. "She may be a bit plain, but she's not *that* bad."

All but Mitch whipped their heads around.

"Plain?" Chase muttered.

"Okay, so she's no looker—" Eve started.

"Or talker," Craig interrupted. "I'm not a complete heathen. A woman doesn't have to look like a movie star to draw my attention, and I can certainly ignore her Victorian taste in fashion with collars up to her neck, sleeves down to her knuckles, and dark colors suitable for a funeral, but it helps if she could carry her half of the conversation. Heck, I would have settled for one-tenth of the conversation."

Mitch, the brother following in the Governor's political footsteps, and the only brother not to react to Eve's earlier comment, pushed to his feet. "Cut Gwyneth some slack. Growing up with Prudence Van Klein as a mother couldn't have been much of a picnic. As I remember it, even as a kid she hated crowds."

"That's right." Kyle snapped his fingers. "Weren't you her escort for her coming-out party a hundred years ago?"

Mitch nodded. "She didn't say a word to me until the end of the night, and even then all she said was *thank you*. But I do remember thinking that her eyes seemed to be saying more."

Chase caught the way his brother Mitch, gazing out the window, appeared to be lost in another place and time. Two years ago his wife had been killed in a car crash. Since then, unless he was in front of a podium or a camera, Mitch always seemed to be somewhere else. "Strange encounters like that are what make my idea for this wedding celebration the perfect plan," Chase continued. "I'll have no worries that a real date will fall in love with the estate, the money, the perks, and come up with heaven-only-knows-what plan to stay in my world. No thank you." They'd all been down that road before, and Chase had run out of financially stable socialites to parade in front of his family.

"So how did you find this woman?" Eve asked.

"Community theater. I arrived in Galveston earlier than expected. When I learned Andrew and Nancy were heading out to see a show at the new theater, I tagged along. That's when I got the idea and approached Bev after the show. She agreed over dinner."

"I don't know." Craig plopped his ankle over his knee.

"No matter what Mitch thinks, I'm certainly not giving the Governor a chance to stick me with a wedding date like Gwyneth Van Klein." Chase kept an eye on the harbor as the captain steered the cabin cruiser into the slip. "What about you?" He lifted his chin at his sister.

"Jack Preston."

"My friend?" Kyle's brows curled into a V. "From college?"

Eve nodded. "He was in town for a conference and we bumped into each other."

Chase leaned forward. He knew the name. Jack was not only a friend from his brother's fraternity, he was also a cohort in crime for Kyle's partying ways. Why hadn't Chase heard about this? "Is it serious?"

"Yeah," Kyle echoed, his tone laced with discontent.

"It's not like that." Eve shook her head.

"So what's it like?"

"Just friends with mutually compatible bank accounts."

"Ah." Relieved, Chase leaned back in his seat. "Leech repellent."

"Oh, I hate it when you say that." Eve set her glass on the table. "When is your date arriving?"

"Soon. She's joining us for dinner." One of the perks of the Baron fortune was Baron Enterprises stable of world wide hotels including the ultra private Galveston seaside resort and golf club.

"I made reservations for all of us on the veranda," Kyle said. "This way everyone can get to spend a little time with Andrew and Nancy before the rest of the clan descends en mass as well as get to know Chase's date better before the Governor arrives tomorrow."

"Sounds like a plan." Chase stood with the rest of his siblings. The cabin cruiser from the yacht had docked, and he was anxious to get this show on the road. He especially wanted to visit a little more with the soon-to-be newest member of the Baron clan. Except for flying down briefly for Andrew's birthday last month, they'd hardly spoken in person. Every time he had arranged to be at the family ranch north of Houston for the Governor's regularly scheduled Sunday dinner on the same date Andrew and Nancy were in attendance, some crisis that only Chase could deal with had come up and kept him away. This time he had vowed, even if the world spun off its axis, he would not miss his cousin's wedding. "Any chance you'll let me drive that little Aston of yours?"

Kyle shook his head back and forth multiple times. "Not in my lifetime."

"Come on. Who taught you how to drive?"

"And *that*"—Kyle raised a finger in the air—"is exactly why you're not driving the Aston."

A few minutes later their various cars pulled into the Gulf Shores Resort and Golf Club. Despite being somewhat isolated and catering to a very small and exclusive clientele, the hotel and the restaurant's reputations were both five star. Chase had been looking forward to relaxing and recharging. Another reason he'd chosen to hire his companion for the week. Trying to please a woman was more work than running a Fortune 500 company. And certainly more exhausting.

"Do you see her?" Eve asked, scanning the crowd in the small restaurant.

"No. But it's still a few minutes before seven."

"Welcome." The chef rushed from the kitchen two steps ahead of the hostess to greet Kyle and the others. "It's always a pleasure to have you dine with us, Mr. Baron. Especially for you, we have added Lobster Thermidor to this evening's menu."

"Superb."

"Carolyn will escort you to your favorite spot on the veranda."

Scanning the surroundings, Chase followed behind, not

paying attention to the chef's recitation of this evening's specials. More than once Kyle had raved about the perfection of the resort remodel and caliber of the restaurant. His brother hadn't exaggerated. The entire resort would easily fit in on any of Chase's favorite islands. Sandy beaches, rushing waters, and, if he were in the market for a woman, prime scantily clad specimens. Too bad this week was intended to be strictly uncomplicated. Beverly Lawson was definitely a looker. Exactly the arm candy his grandfather would expect his grandsons to be seen with. And, fortunately, not one Chase would be expected to marry. Though hopefully, if Beverly did her job right, the Governor wouldn't figure that out until after the reception and Chase's flight back to Dallas.

The high standards the Governor expected every Baron descendant to follow quickly culled the pool of prospective spouses. Lila, Chase's grandmother, had been the daughter of a general. The Governor claimed to have fallen in love with her the moment she had walked into the room at her father's side. It was Lila Baron's maternal side of the family who had their roots in Texas Ranch country. The combination of military and ranch life left their grandmother used to hard work and strict discipline. A woman who could wrangle a calf or host a state dinner with her eyes closed, his Grams had set the standard every Baron offspring was expected to follow in finding a mate. A task Chase's father, the youngest of the Governor's sons, had failed at—three times. The fourth yet to be determined.

The Governor had originally approved of Millicent Bainbridge Baron, Chase's mother, or at least of her pedigree. However, after bearing Chase's father four healthy sons and a daughter, his mom proved to be emotionally incapable of surviving the Governor's military harshness, coupled with her husband's propensity for skirt-chasing. By the time Eve, the youngest offspring from his union with Millicent, was in school, their father had moved on to wife number two. It hadn't taken much time for him to move on to number three. By then Millicent had become a social recluse. When Eve graduated from high school, their mom had finally had enough, packed up all her treasures, sold the handsome home she'd been left in the very untidy Baron divorce, and dug year long into her favorite summer home in the Belgian countryside.

Glancing at his computerized watch, Chase hoped Beverly wouldn't be one of those women who believed in keeping a man waiting. For what she was costing him, she'd better understand that, when he said 7:00 p.m., he didn't mean 7:05.

"Excuse me, sir." The pretty young hostess stood awkwardly between him and Kyle. "A woman is asking for Mr. Chase Baron."

Exactly 7:00 p.m. on the nose. This was going to be an easy week. "That would be me." Chase pushed to his feet and walked into the main restaurant. Beverly might be getting paid for her services, but that didn't mean he could let decades of good breeding fall by the wayside. A man never left a lady standing alone, waiting. Except the only person standing alone was not Beverly Lawson. Tall with short chin-length brown hair, the stranger stood ramrod straight, and her expression told him she was less-than-pleased to be here.

Years of training told him to turn around and let the staff handle this, but an instinct deep in his gut propelled him toward the unhappy woman. "I'm Chase Baron."

CHAPTER THREE

C.J. had to be out of her ever-loving mind. The idea of hiring out as a date for a billionaire was insane. The Cinderella *happily ever afters* her sister loved so much only happened in movies. With C.J.'s luck, she'd wind up chained to a bed, like in a *Criminal Minds* episode. For a precious hour she and her sister had argued that very point. But—with debt out the wazoo and the carrot of an expensive trip to Canada dangling in front of Bev—in the end, C.J. had agreed to do what she'd done her whole life: help her sister out of a jam. After all, better for a battle-trained Marine to take on whatever kind of lunatic her baby sister had gotten entangled with than for her delicate dreamer of a sister. Since most of the clothes in CJ's closet consisted of desert camo, she had spent another hour picking out an affordable dress that didn't make her feel like a Barbie doll and these ridiculous strappy heels the sales girl had talked her into.

Standing in the foyer of what was clearly a very expensive restaurant, C.J. ignored the prickly feeling in her gut that warned of impending danger. Instead, she focused on the young hostess who had promised to fetch Mr. Baron. Mentally strong, C.J. liked to think herself prepared, but the man walking toward her had *T-R-O-U-B-L-E* emblazoned across his forehead. And not the sort she'd anticipated. Light chestnut hair cut just above his collar gleamed under the overhead lights. Dark blue eyes teetering on steel gray could no doubt charm a snake. But his broad shoulders and well-muscled body made her pulse rate jump. The words *power*, *money*, and *Roman god* came to mind. One she was committed to spending an entire week with, playing coy and cute.

Not that *coy* or *cute* were in her vocabulary. Fresh out of high school she'd gone straight to the recruiting office and signed on the dotted line. Early on she'd learned that fitting in meant being one of the guys. She could carry a full-load pack across a five-mile swamp, shoot a bull's-eye dead center every time, and yet walking five feet in three-inch heels got the better of her. *Cute* and *coy* were not going to happen.

"I'm Chase Baron."

C.J. stuck out her hand and did her best to put on a confident smile. "C. J. Lawson reporting for duty." Oh, what an idiot she was. "I'm your date."

Up close his eyes burned an even deeper blue-gray. His glance momentarily shot over her shoulder and back before he accepted her proffered hand. His grip was strong but not bone-crushing. She'd have to add *confident* to the other descriptions already tumbling about in her mind.

His eyes did a quick perusal from head to toe and back. "I'm afraid there's been a mistake."

"No mistake." The urge to squirm under his scrutiny nearly had her shifting in place. He would have made a good drill sergeant, but, if Mr. Baron wanted to play a staring game, she could give as good as she got.

A couple with two teens came in the front door, breaking the silent spell. Without a second's hesitation Chase linked his hand around her arm, led her across the spacious entry, and out the side door. He didn't stop walking until he reached a secluded corner of the beach deck. "Where is Beverly?"

"On her way to Canada."

Only the momentary tensing of his jaw gave away any sign of irritation. Chase was one cool cucumber. "And you are?"

"Her sister. Bev explained you need someone to pretend to be your date for a wedding. I can do that."

"You're an actress?"

C.J. shook her head. "I'm ... between jobs." Not the whole truth but not a lie.

Chase blew out a heavy breath. "How much did your sister tell you?"

Not nearly enough. "That you want your grandfather to believe you're in a relationship."

Again his gaze studied hers; only for a second did he glance away to take in the happenings around the room, and yet she would have made odds that he knew exactly what was going on everywhere, down to the tiniest detail.

"Chase." Another tall, good-looking man, clearly poured from the same mold, came up beside him. "Eve just hung up with Grams. The limo turned onto the seawall a few minutes ago. They'll be here any second."

"Thanks." Only a slight twitch at his jaw line showed his displeasure at the news.

The Chase clone extended his hand to her. "I'm Kyle Baron. You must be my big brother's new lady." He gave her a conspiratorial wink. "Nice to meet you."

"How do you do? C. J. Lawson." Another firm and controlled handshake. Were they all a force to be reckoned with?

Kyle smiled and nodded at his brother. "Not what I expected. You may just pull this off." Without any response from Chase, Kyle turned on his heel and made his way around the corner.

"Well, C.J."—Chase spun about to face her—"it looks like you're hired."

Some days Chase wondered if his grandfather's only pleasure in life was making his grandchildren squirm. The Governor was a walking poster for *Once a Marine, Always a Marine*. Anything that kept his family tough and on their toes fit perfectly in the Governor's plans. But his early arrival didn't give Chase any time to learn enough about this woman to properly prepare. At least with Bev, they'd talked a bit and had a logical story of how they'd met. With C.J., he'd have to come up with some meet-cute they'd both have to remember. The best deceptions were built on truths. Total fabrications too easily led to trouble.

"Does he do this often?" C.J. asked, interrupting his thoughts.

"The Governor, yes. And we don't have much time. Let's get introductions to the rest of my siblings over with before my grandfather arrives. We'll work out the backstory later."

"I gather they know what's going on?"

"Of course. We'll have to wing it through dinner. I'll make an excuse to slip away early, before the Governor has time to interrogate you."

"I can hold my own."

Standing rigid, her chin rose up, and he realized now what he had assumed to be nerves was pure gumption. A part of him almost smiled. His grandfather loved gumption, but Chase's inner businessman reminded him that this was merely a game of pretend. In the long run what his grandfather thought wouldn't matter. Resting his hand along the small of her back, Chase ignored the way she'd stiffened and nudged her forward.

His brothers stood to greet C.J.

"Hello. I'm Craig."

"And I'm Mitch."

Kyle just smiled.

"Pleasure to meet you." She nodded.

"We'd better move this along," Chase interrupted. "I'll need you guys to run interference for us this evening. Since I thought we'd have a full twenty-four hours, I haven't had time to properly prep C.J."

Mitch rolled his eyes at the same moment the repetitive clack of the Governor's cane echoed through the restaurant.

Leaning into his new date, Chase whispered in her ear, "Rushing up to my grandmother, is my sister Eve. The baby."

C.J.'s eyes remained pinned to Eve, running into her grandmother's embrace. "I'm guessing your sister doesn't see it that way."

It took a second for Chase to consider C.J.'s words. A simple concept really; and yet, to him, even after the birth of his half sisters, Eve was still his baby sister. "No, I suppose she doesn't."

"And where is the woman who finally caught one of my grandchildren?" the Governor bellowed.

"I'm right here." A woman came hurrying across the deck. "Sorry I'm late."

Andrew scooped his fiancée into his side and softly exchanged words no one else was meant to hear. Nancy smiled and nodded, and, for a split second, Chase felt a pang of envy to find a woman who would look at him and not his money with such adoration.

"Tardiness is not something to strive for." The General stared Nancy down.

Lifting her chin and straightening her shoulders, Nancy managed a soft smile. "Agreed, but my grandmother's health is declining. Family is always a priority."

The Governor stared down his nose at her for a long minute before nodding. "Agreed."

In unison, every Baron sibling exhaled a long-held breath. Chase wanted to pat his cousin on the back and bow to his future cousin-in-law. That tiny sliver of envy quickly swelled. Surely another woman somewhere on this planet could love him for himself and stand strong under the heavy mantle of the Baron dynasty.

"By the way"—the Governor waited until Nancy and his wife were seated to speak—"I've invited a few additional people to the wedding. A last-minute thing. I hope you don't mind."

Nancy's eyes flashed with surprise before a curtain of calm descended. "I'm sure we can work in a few extra people."

"Good." The Governor sat. "The Kessler sisters will be joining us. I thought it would be nice to sit the older one with Porter and the younger with"—his eyes flickered to Chase, then C.J., and back—"Colton."

Nancy looked to Kyle, who rolled his eyes and glanced at Chase.

Had he called it or what? C.J. had just saved him from a week with another one of the Governor's *suitable* candidates for Baronhood.

CHAPTER FOUR

"**A**nother wonderful dinner." The Governor pulled the chair out for his wife. "The driver is waiting, and it's a long ride home."

C.J. smiled up at the older couple. The dinner had gone much better than she'd anticipated. Champagne, wine, and whiskey had flowed like water. The tab might very well have equaled her pay for an entire month. Shrimp, lobster, and prime-cut steaks were the main entrées of choice, with hers being the only order of chicken. Not a single person batted an eye at the amount of food coming from the kitchen or the mounting bill.

"Are you sure you wouldn't prefer to check in straightaway to the resort tonight?" Chase asked his grandfather, pushing away from the table.

"Yes." the Governor nodded. "We'll move into our suite after the family dinner to be closer to all the festivities."

Following his grandfather's lead, Andrew pulled out the chair for his fiancée.

"Have we given any thought to a honeymoon baby?"

"Governor," Lila Baron interrupted her husband.

"Yes, dear." All discussion of plans of babies ended.

As soon as the Governor and their grandmother were out of sight, Craig slapped his eldest brother on the back. "Looks like you pulled it off."

"With everyone's help." Chase looked to his sister and

brothers. "A Baron team effort."

"We did do a great job of casually redirecting the Governor's attention." Eve took the last sip of her wine, set the glass on the table, and slung her purse strap over her shoulder. "I have to admit it was kind of fun pulling one over on the old warhorse. A little thrilling actually."

"I'm not sure I understand." C.J. reached for her own purse. "He seemed like a perfectly charming old man."

"As long as you're doing what he wants," Craig said, "the Governor can be more than charming. But heaven forbid you don't do things his way."

"Fifteen last-minute guests." Nancy shook her head at her future husband. "All to be dispersed among the family. I hope the wedding planner doesn't kill me."

"Told ya." Chase chuckled. "The man is on a mission. You single guys need to plan ahead or prepare to be steamrolled straight to the altar."

"And this, my dear brother"—Craig gave an exaggerated bow—"is why you run Baron Enterprises. You may be the only one in the family who can stay one step ahead of the old man."

Chase laughed at his brother's antics, while Mitch remained a silent observer.

"So," Craig continued, "now that the show is over, are we heading back to the Baroness or hanging out here for another drink?"

"*The Baroness?*" C.J. had actually said very little most of the evening. She'd found it fascinating listening to the conversations about everything from politics to racing sailboats, of which the family apparently owned several. But she'd thought all the family members were staying here at the resort.

"Kyle's yacht," Craig answered. "The siblings are hiding out from reality there for another night before moving to the resort."

"I'm ready to call it a night." Mitch rolled his neck and offered a wan smile.

"It'll be a long week. I'll meet you guys there." Chase turned to C.J. "Where's your bag?"

"Bag?"

"Luggage?" He shrugged.

"Luggage?"

His gaze narrowed. "Why are you repeating everything I say?"

"I don't need a bag or luggage."

"Are you planning on wearing this dress all week?"

"Of course not."

"Then what do you usually transport your clothing in?"

A duffel bag. "Why am I transporting clothes?"

For a long moment Chase stared at her, as though she'd spoken in a foreign language. "Because you're staying on the *Baroness* with me."

"The heck I am." Her sister hadn't been sure what the plans were, but C.J. wasn't her sister. "I see no reason I can't commute back and forth when I'm needed."

"The arrangement with your sister was for her to stay on the *Baroness* until we all move to the resort."

"I repeat, I see no reason I can't commute."

"If you have a problem with staying on a boat, I can assure you it's as stable and comfortable as anywhere on dry land."

"I don't have a problem with water." Heaven knows she'd ridden on every type of transport known to man on land, sea, and air. "I'd prefer to commute."

Chase ran his hand across the back of his neck, then let it fall to his side on a sigh. "That won't work. It will be harder to convince the Governor that we're a couple if he learns you live here in Houston since I live in Dallas. Besides, the schedule this week is packed, starting with a family dinner Sunday evening at Baron ranch, followed by a high tea on Monday. Then a luncheon at Nancy's mother's country club on Wednesday, as well as dinner for the bridesmaids and a few other girlfriends, including you—"

"Me? I'm not a part of this."

"This week you are." Chase rattled off an even longer list of events, covering just about every minute of every day right up to the wedding ceremony next Saturday night. "So you see, it will be much easier for sanity's sake to have you nearby."

"And where would I be sleeping?" She might as well lay her cards on the table.

A sly grin teased at one corner of his mouth. "I don't need to buy that sort of companionship."

C.J. didn't respond. He was probably right, but, since she didn't really know this man, what did he expect for his ten thousand dollars?

"It's a big yacht and a big resort. Either way you'll have your own room."

"Fine. I can drive home tonight and throw a few things in a bag and return tomorrow."

Chase ran his hand over his face, and, for the first time all evening, she noticed how tired he looked. Not just from a long night but his eyes held a weariness that came from more than a single long day. "Let's do this," he said. "I'll follow you home. I have a few calls I can make while you pack, and then I'll help with your bags."

"That won't be necessary. I don't have much to pack so it won't take me long, and I certainly don't need you to tag along simply to carry my suitcase." Even if she had a massive wardrobe, she could handle this on her own.

Chase studied her again, and C.J. got the feeling he was carefully considering his next words. "I must admit, I've never known a woman who could pack a week's worth of clothes, including attire for two formal dinners, quickly."

"Formal?"

"The wedding is black tie."

She probably should have realized the main event would be formal. But why two gowns? Immediately her mind jumped to her bank balance. She'd hoped to stretch her savings until she'd had time to decide about her future; eveningwear didn't come cheap. "Why two?"

"Special event family dinners with the Governor are always an occasion for formal dress. The upcoming wedding makes tomorrow's dinner a special event." Slipping his hand around the small of her back, he nudged her forward. "Let's finish this conversation on the way to your house."

"Apartment. It's Bev's." That was a stupid thing to say, but her mind scrambled to organize all the details she hadn't considered when she'd agreed to fill in for her sister. Apparently C.J. had a lot more to worry about than whose bed she would be expected to sleep in.

The flaws in Chase's brilliant but hasty plan were beginning to show. It had never crossed his mind that Beverly, or in this case C.J., would think he'd expect sex as part of the business agreement. Sex had a way of complicating things, and the last thing he wanted was complicated. Assuming that a community theater actress, never mind a last-minute substitute, would have a wardrobe suitable for any major Baron family event was another glaring misstep on his part.

"If you let me have your garment sizes, I can have a personal shopper pick out a few things for you to wear this week."

C.J.'s steps slowed. "Personal shopper?"

Was he mumbling? Babbling in tongues? Why did she repeat everything he said in the form of a question? "I'm sure Eve can recommend someone suitable in the area."

"I don't think I can do that."

"It's quite easy. We use them all the time. Certainly makes shopping for Christmas and birthday gifts much easier."

"I'm sure it's quite easy, but no one has picked out my clothes for me since I was a toddler. I'd feel like a Barbie doll if someone tried to dress me like your sister." C.J. felt the heat of embarrassment rise to her cheeks. "That didn't come out right. What I mean is, trendy fashions look great on someone lean and sophisticated, such as Eve, but I'd feel like a kid playing dress up—badly—if someone outfitted me like a cover model."

Until now he hadn't given much thought to C.J.'s appearance. She looked nothing like her sister. Where Bev was a head-turning petite blue-eyed sunshine blonde with long hair worthy of a shampoo commercial, C.J. was tall, of average weight but on the sturdy side, with short light-brown hair and eyes the color of dark chocolate. At first sight she didn't leave much of an impression, but, now that he took a moment to really look at her, she reminded him of a young Demi Moore with natural sun-kissed highlights. That embarrassed flush softened her hard edges. Under the gruff demeanor, C. J. Lawson was an attractive woman. "I'm sure you'll look lovely in whatever you wear."

"Thank you, but trust me on this. I'm not high-fashion material." She blew out a soft sigh that suddenly left him very aware of how closely they stood.

Her gaze flickered left, then right. He could see her mind analyzing, debating, and then her moment of decision. This sudden change in casting could prove to be interesting. Unlike his original lead for this week's production, C.J. was both pretty and smart.

Standing straight with resignation, C.J. nodded. "It does, however, look like I'll need to get a few things for the rest of the week."

"All right. If the personal shopper is out, how about I pick you up tomorrow morning around ten? We'll shop for whatever you need and then check into the resort. Sound like a plan?"

Her brown eyes narrowed in thought, and he found himself holding his breath, waiting for her answer. On another soft sigh, she nodded her head. "Ten o'clock."

"Ten o'clock," he repeated, plastering on his encouraging smile. At least one of them should look pleased about shopping. Even if, like everything else about this week, it was all just for show.

CHAPTER FIVE

With every passing moment C.J. was more convinced of her unsound mind. *Shopping*. Her closet consisted mostly of uniforms, and, when she did wear civvies, she relied on a few pairs of jeans and a collection of comfy T-shirts she'd accumulated through the years. As it was, yesterday she'd sifted through racks of discounted clothes for a dress to wear last night before finding something. The simple straight-lined dress didn't make her look like a kid playing dress up, but fit in with the sort of people who could afford thousands of dollars for a date. At least she hoped it had. After all, what the heck did she know about people with enough cash to use hundred dollar bills for kindling?

Nonetheless, at 9:55 a.m., she and her carry-on bag—filled with little more than underwear and toiletries—waited for Chase to arrive. In complete contrast to how little she looked forward to hitting a department store, she was definitely more enthused than she should be about seeing Chase again. Their arrangement was strictly business—and by default no less. He'd wanted to play footsie—or at least pretend to—with her sister. Not with her.

So why did she feel a tiny rush of anticipation waiting for the man? Another stupid question. How about because she was a red-blooded female and Chase was handsome enough to make that red blood sizzle. Or maybe it had something to do with the end of the previous evening, when he had looked at her like she was a desirable woman. After years of blending into a man's world, C.J. had almost forgotten she wasn't a man.

The trill of the doorbell pulled her back to reality. A day of shopping mall hell. For a foolish moment as she opened the door, she wondered if there was such a thing as a camo evening gown.

On the other side of the threshold, Chase stood, smiling. Charm and charisma oozed from his pores. She had to wonder why a man with so much natural sex appeal needed to pay for a date, though he had clearly stated he did not need to buy intimate companionship. Hiring Bev made no sense.

"Ready?" he asked.

"All set." She raised her bag to show him and almost bolted backward from his touch when he tried to take it from her. "I can handle it."

"I'm sure you can, but that's not the point." His smile widened in complete contradiction to his pointed gaze. "Besides," he continued, "my grandfather would never let me hear the end of it if he knew I let you carry your own bag."

The urge to let his hand remain on hers for the rest of the day was why she relented. Keeping a safe distance just became a priority. "There's a nice mall not far from here. They have some good sales going on."

Reaching the car a few steps ahead of her, Chase nodded and opened the passenger door. She could see his eyes daring her to object. She knew when to pick her battles. This wasn't one of them. Sliding inside, she strapped in and waited for him to toss her bag in the back and take his place behind the wheel. Then the engine roared to life.

"Turn left at the end of the road." She pointed ahead. "A couple of lights later you'll see the signs for the freeway."

"Actually"—Chase shifted gears and took a second to flash her a wily grin—"Eve recommended a place she thought would work."

Like C.J. could afford anywhere a Baron shopped. "I really think the mall will be—"

"C.J.," he interrupted, his gaze softer, "let me handle this. Please."

She had the strangest feeling that the *please* had been hard for him to say. Something she didn't think he did often. And something she couldn't say no to. Even if her credit card might not agree.

Eve had told Chase that Le Magasin would be the perfect one-stop place to take C.J. shopping without trying his patience. Driving his brother's Mercedes sedan with the plates BARON II, it was no surprise to Chase when he pulled up to the door that the valet addressed him by name. When the shop manager greeted him at the door, he knew his sister had phoned ahead.

"Good morning, Mr. Baron. My name is Marguerite." The picture-perfect woman—anywhere from thirty to fifty years old, depending on her genetics or plastic surgeon—introduced herself. Walking beside her, a younger but equally well-dressed woman waited to be introduced. "This is Veronica. She will be taking care of you today."

Veronica looked C.J. up and down. "Size 8?"

C.J. tightened the two-fisted grip on her purse strap. "Ten actually."

"We'll try both. Most of the clothing from our designers tends to run smaller than … other brands."

While Veronica had maintained a steady tone and pleasant smile, he didn't need to be at the helm of a multibillion-dollar company, nor carry the weight of the Baron name, to recognize the sales girl had very politely but disrespectfully put C.J. in her bargain-shopper place. And he didn't like it one little bit.

"Very well," the manager said, waving toward a small lounge with scattered seating and a single door leading to what he knew to be a private dressing room. "I will leave you in Veronica's competent hands."

He had to think fast. "Thank you, but my sister mentioned another name." Eve had, of course, said nothing about which salesperson she used or if she even had a preferred individual at the store, but this wouldn't be the first time Chase had tossed out a vague presumption in hopes of luring in wanted information.

"I see." The older woman looked to Veronica, then back at Chase. "I do believe Melissa usually works with your sister, but she's with another customer."

Chase didn't move, didn't say a word. He let his silence hang for a long uncomfortable moment, and then, when he could see the manager's confident gaze begin to mire with concern, he added, "Perhaps we should come back another time."

With only a gentle nod in Veronica's direction, Marguerite had made her decision. Veronica slipped quietly from the room. "That won't be necessary, Mr. Baron," the manager continued. "If you'll have a seat, I'm sure we can arrange for Melissa to assist Miss ..."

"Lawson," C.J. supplied.

"May I offer you some refreshment while you wait? A cup of tea perhaps? Or something cold?"

Rigidly standing in place, C.J.'s nearly white-knuckled hold on her bag was his only clue that she wasn't as calm as she might appear to a casual stranger.

"Nothing for me, thank you," she said.

He didn't know much about C.J., not even her full name

he realized, but he recognized she was uncomfortable as all get out, and yet she'd calmly responded and even managed a smile. Pretty, smart, *and* tough.

"And you, Mr. Baron?" Marguerite asked.

"No, thank you." He forced his focus from C.J. "Nothing for me either."

"Very well."

Once the woman was out of sight, Chase turned to C.J. "We might as well sit down."

The way she looked down at the chairs, he'd have thought snakes lay curled there, waiting to strike.

"I'm sure we could have found something at the mall."

"This will be faster." He gestured for her to take a seat.

Relinquishing the death grip on her bag, C.J. eased into the chair.

"What's your full name?"

Her shoulders relaxed. "Cassandra Jane."

"Cassandra. That's a lovely name. Why do you hide behind your initials?"

On a heavy sigh, she answered, "Most of my adult life I've lived in a man's world. Cassandra or even Cassie brought more femininity to the table than I wanted to deal with. C.J. was simply easier."

That could explain the tough shell C.J. wore like a shield. He realized now exactly how little he really knew about her. "What sort of work is it you do?"

"I'm a nurse. I've recently—"

"So sorry to keep you waiting." A young woman with an infectious smile came calmly rushing into the lounge and extended a hand to C.J. first, then Chase. "I'm Missy. I can't tell you how pleased I am to meet one of Miss Baron's brothers and Miss Lawson." Without waiting for Chase to respond, she spun around to face C.J., then slapped her hands together and rubbed enthusiastically. "So, are we ready to have some fun?"

CHAPTER SIX

Fun would be the last word C.J. would have chosen to describe the torture of shopping, especially today, but at least she already liked Missy much better than Veronica. For one thing Missy didn't look at C.J. as though she were a piece of chewing gum stuck to the sole of her Ferragamo's.

"What are we wanting today?" Missy asked.

Resigned to whatever was coming next, C.J. rose from her chair. "I need two formal dresses."

"Shoes and purses to match also," Chase added. "As well as a couple of outfits suitable for sailing—"

"Sailing?" C.J. interrupted.

"I think that's Thursday afternoon. You don't get seasick, do you?"

She shook her head. It was easier than reminding him that he'd already asked that question last night.

"Good. Miss Lawson will also be attending a barbecue."

"Barbecue?"

Chase nodded and continued, "The bachelorette party." He paused a split second, as though expecting her to interrupt, but C.J. must have already figured out there was no point in doing so. He apparently hadn't exaggerated at all when he said she had a busy week ahead of her. "A rehearsal dinner and ..." He paused to glance at her, his gaze soft, appreciative. "And a dinner date at Casa Bodega this evening."

Already anxious just anticipating the plethora of engagements to play her part as Chase Baron's date, her heart stuttered at the way his gaze locked with hers when he announced dinner tonight. Nothing about his words sounded very businesslike or wedding related. To her rusty instincts, the statement almost sounded like he'd invited her on a real date.

"We'd better get started then." Missy took a step back. "If you'll come with me a moment, I'll show you a few things to get a feel for your taste, and then I can take over from there."

Moving away from Chase Baron was probably a good thing. She didn't like the way her skin tingled every time he looked her way. She wasn't the tingly sort of person, and she couldn't let all of this Cinderella treatment blind her to reality. This was a job. A short-term job. One that ended next Sunday morning when Chase Baron flew to his luxurious lifestyle in Dallas while she returned to her sister's one-bedroom rented apartment.

Across the hall, Missy brought C.J. into a circular room. A couple of comfortable leather chairs anchored the center, and loosely filled racks fit into smaller sections of the walls. Missy walked diagonally across the space toward a handful of gowns. She bypassed the few glistening with beads and bangles and instead reached for a one-shoulder dark purple dress that looked awfully good on the satin hanger.

"This should be quite flattering with your figure." Missy pulled it off the rack and held it out for C.J. to approve. "This also comes with a large floral applique on the shoulder, but you don't strike me as the sort to appreciate extra bling."

"Good call. No bling."

Missy's smile brightened. She returned the dress to the rack, and C.J. did her best to finger what she thought might be a price tag while Missy moved to another section of clothes. However, the only numbers had to be a model number of some kind, because, if it were the cost of the dress, C.J. would need a bank loan to pay for the thing.

"Mr. Baron didn't mention what the bachelorette event entails. What sort of outfit did you have in mind?"

"Beats me."

Rather than looking down her nose at C.J. the way Veronica might have done, Missy smothered another smile. "Personally I think the world would be happier if we all could just live and work in sweats."

"Exactly. Though on the Gulf Coast I'd prefer my gym shorts and a T-shirt."

"I don't know that we can pull that off for girls' night, but ..." Missy curled her forefinger for C.J. to follow. At the end of the hall they stepped into another circular room, only this one was clearly meant to be the rich and famous's idea of sportswear. "White is usually the color of preference on a sailboat around here, but I find it tedious to launder." Missy held out a pair of khaki shorts and what C.J. could best describe as a matching glorified T-shirt with splotches of sea blue.

"So far that's the only thing I've seen that I might actually wear again."

"Miss Baron loves this designer. She reminds me a lot of you."

"Me?" What the heck could a former medic-turned-registered-nurse, raised in the low-rent district, possibly have in common with Eve Baron was beyond her.

"You both have a subtle beauty that doesn't need all the trappings most of my clients rely on. I don't think I've ever seen Miss Baron come in here wearing makeup or expensive jewelry. Seeing her on the streets, you'd never know she comes from one of the top ten richest families in the world."

Top ten? All the saliva in C.J.'s mouth suddenly evaporated.

"No one would know who her brother is."

"Which brother?"

Missy hesitated, her eyes darting around the room. C.J. got the impression she hadn't meant to say anything. "Kyle."

"I don't understand."

"Well, you know." She glanced around again. "His nickname and all."

C.J. raised a brow.

"I'm sorry. I thought everyone knew."

"I've been overseas a very long time. I don't hear much."

Missy nodded and lowered her voice. "Knockout Kyle. Hardly a day goes by that Kyle Baron doesn't turn up on the cover of some rag magazine at the grocery store."

The only thing C.J. knew about Kyle Baron was that he loved his cars, his boats, and so far had been perfectly polite and respectable around her. Kyle's conversation last night had circled mostly around dinner, his younger siblings, and sailing with the occasional comment about politics or sports. C.J. couldn't see scandal rags anywhere in that family picture. "What about the other brothers? Are they popular in the news too?"

"Couldn't say. Usually it's Kyle who does something to put the family in the spotlight. Eve occasionally mentioned the others in passing. I think she worries most about the Senator."

"Senator?" Holy combat boots. Brother Mitch sitting beside her at dinner was *Senator* Mitchell Baron. Crud. How had it escaped her that she was spending the week with the closest thing to American royalty since the Kennedys?

The plans for tonight were supposed to be dinner with his brothers and sister on the *Baroness,* then tomorrow he'd be attending the family dinner along with any cousins, aunts, and uncles who were already in town for the wedding. Dinner at Casa Bodega for just him and C.J. was not on the tightly packed schedule. The intriguing contrast of sweet chocolate-brown eyes and her stalwart effort to fit in had the invitation slipping from his lips before he had time to give any serious thought to the consequences of dinner for two. Though, on a practical note, tonight could be used to solidify their story, should the Governor get her alone. Hearing footsteps, he glanced up in time to see C.J. coming down the hall, a cup in each hand.

Her stride was wide, pounding, and determined. "I think I may have given Veronica another reason to boot me out of this place as a trespasser."

"What did she do?" Chase was almost to his feet when C.J. shook her head and shoved a hot mug in his face, urging him back to his seat.

"I hope you like coffee. You didn't strike me as a tea person. And to answer your question, Veronica didn't do a thing. I refused to let one of the café workers bring us the coffee."

"What do you mean, *refused*?"

"I was standing right there." C.J.'s voice rose half an octave. "I insisted I could carry the coffee myself. Veronica may have glanced in my direction at exactly the moment I'd repeated I could certainly carry my own coffee. I mean, seriously? Doesn't it strike you as a little absurd to walk away and have someone else bring me the coffee, when, if I waited another thirty seconds for them to pour the cup, I could bring it myself? Really just ten if you don't count the twenty seconds it took to argue the point."

A still small voice deep in the back of his head screamed this was a test. "Perhaps."

Her gaze narrowed, and he got the distinct impression he'd given the wrong answer.

"If you want milk or sugar, you'll have to go get them."

"No." He didn't see the point in mentioning that, regardless of her insistence, shop personnel would come along any second and check on them. It was how things worked in his world. Occasionally to the point of wait staff becoming a nuisance. "Black is fine." Looking over the rim of his cup, he noticed she drank hers black as well. That had him wondering what part of a man's world did she live in?

"Are you ready?" Missy stood in front of them, empty-handed. "If you'll follow me to the dressing area, you can try on what I've chosen for you."

Chase sat back and took another sip of his coffee. He wished he could have seen C.J. standing her ground. She was proving to be nothing like he expected. Most women would have fallen all over themselves for the wardrobe he offered to buy, and yet she honestly didn't seem to want it. What he thought of as a little stubborn, she probably saw as independent. Either way, it was a breath of fresh air from the plastic women who passed through his life. He'd finished his coffee, and one of the café staff had, indeed, come by to see if he wanted another cup. He'd almost finished his second cup when the door to C.J.'s changing room finally opened.

"I was beginning to think I wouldn't see ..." His last words slipped away. Producing a coherent sentence was no longer an option. C.J. looked absolutely stunning. He'd guessed her height yesterday to be around five seven or eight, and he knew she wasn't of a delicate frame, but yesterday's loose-fitting dress and today's jeans and T-shirt hadn't prepared him for the luscious shape standing before him draped in a royal purple gown. "You look … lovely."

So stunned with her entrance, he hadn't noticed the apprehension on her face until he saw it slide away, making room for a tentative smile and a spark of satisfaction in her eyes. "It doesn't look bad, does it?"

"You'll be the most beautiful woman in the room."

A hint of pink rose to her cheeks, and she quickly spun about to face the three-way mirror. He supposed it was another mechanism for fitting in. The standard rule for success in a man's world: never let them see you sweat. For a woman he supposed he'd have to add: and never let them see you blush.

Watching her turn left, then right, showing off every soft curve, had blood rushing uncomfortably away from his brain. One layered swatch of fabric hung over a shoulder, exposing well-toned arms that showed strength while remaining most definitely feminine. The flow of material drew his gaze across to the soft bare shoulder and then back down the slightest hint of cleavage to where the gown hugged an hourglass figure before breaking loose in smooth flowing waves to the floor. He had no business letting his mind wander to what was under all those layers of purple. Especially since he'd assured her no monkey business. Him and his bright ideas.

CHAPTER SEVEN

Much to C.J.'s surprise, Missy had found C.J. several casual outfits that didn't make her feel like a character in a theatrical production. Currently she had on the softest, most comfortable pair of slacks she'd ever worn. For almost an hour she'd tried to find the price on the clothes she'd been slipping on and off and finally sidled up to Chase. "I don't see the prices. How do I know what they cost?"

"You don't," he deadpanned.

Talking through a toothy smile so as not to draw Missy's attention, C.J. angled her shoulder away from the sales girl. "I have a limited budget." Technically she didn't have any budget at all, but she did have fairly good credit. There wasn't much call for a MasterCard in Kabul.

"Then it's a good thing I don't."

He flashed her one of his high-wattage smiles that she'd gotten used to seeing as she'd come out in outfit after outfit.

"Call it the cost of doing business," he added.

And just like that she'd been snapped out of her Cinderella moment and came crashing down on a rotten pumpkin. This was all business. Fancy clothes were merely the uniform of the day. Petty cash for a Baron.

"Thank you." Swallowing the bitter taste in her mouth, she put on a smile. "So where to now?"

"I'm starved. We'll grab a late lunch, then hit the resort. By the time we arrive, your new clothes should have been delivered to the suite."

"I don't need a suite. A simple room will do."

"We don't have a choice. The resort is sold out. My brother Craig booked the siblings and the Governor the best suites before the rest of the extended family could snatch them up."

"But I'm not a sibling."

"At the time I didn't know I'd have a plus one but don't fret. Our deal is still intact. Most of the suites are as big as small houses with more than one bedroom."

Yes. Their business deal. "If the suite has more than one bedroom, why do you each need your own? Why not share?" The question seemed as practical to her as why shouldn't she wait to carry her own coffee, but, from the look on Chase's face, she might as well have been asking for the mathematical formula for the Pythagorean Theorem.

"Let's just say privacy is important to my family."

The unexpectedly serious expression that took over his face had her thinking maybe all the brothers were closet Knock-out Barons.

The restaurant of choice for their late lunch was not far from the resort. She didn't have to know anything about the place to recognize it would not have a blue-jeans-and-sneakers type of menu. The parking lot was nearly empty, and yet Chase pulled up to valet parking. Thousands of children were starving in the world, but the Barons couldn't walk ten feet to park their own car.

Her door opened, and a good-looking guy held out his hand to her. She'd barely gotten one foot out the door when Chase handed off his keys and extended his elbow to her. A crackle of electricity shot down her arm to rather embarrassing places, and she scolded herself. *Only business.*

"I ate here on my last visit. You'll love the food."

She didn't doubt it. Finding expensive food that was delicious shouldn't be tough. The trick was finding the special epicurean treat for the price of cheap hash. Like everyone else today, once inside, the hostess greeted Chase by name. Was there any place in this world where no one knew who he was? How would this guy handle being treated like an ordinary Joe? To have to wait for a table or search through sales racks in a crowded department store, unable to find a clerk to ring up the sale? How would he handle coming home from months of sleeping in tents fully dressed and armed—in case the need to spring awake struck in the middle of the night—to find he couldn't sleep in the quiet of his own house, the softness of his own bed? Or worse, coming home to no job, no wife, or a home he could no longer live in because it wasn't handicap-friendly?

"Where did you go?" Chase waved his fingers in front of her face.

C.J. looked around. They were seated at a secluded corner table for two with sweeping views of the gulf. Water had been served, and she held the menu in front of her, yet all she could see were the faces of the boys she'd sent home in less-than-perfect shape. "I'm sorry. I guess my mind wandered."

"Give us a few more minutes," he instructed the waiter patiently standing beside the table then Chase skewered her with a questioning glare. "Wherever you wandered off to wasn't a pleasant place."

"Why do you say that?"

He lifted his chin and pointed at her menu. Her grip had tightened to the point of turning her knuckles a creamy white and creasing the plastic-coated menu beneath them. Setting aside the menu, she folded her hands in her lap. "Not every place in this world is pleasant."

"I'm sorry." The intensity in his gaze shifted from curious concern to pained empathy. The sincerity in his gaze, his strength, his compassion, offered her a sliver of comfort she hadn't felt in a very long time.

"Thank you." It wasn't fair of her to paint him with such a harsh brush for having the unique circumstances of being born more than a little wealthy and equally handsome and charming. There was definitely much more to this perceptive man with comfort and compassion in his eyes.

Chase had hoped to learn more about C.J. over lunch, but, after losing her briefly to someplace dark, he feared the wrong question would send her back. Instead he kept the conversation light and breezy. He now knew she'd enjoyed her fish, liked her new slacks, that the khaki shorts were her favorite purchase, and she didn't drink wine in the middle of the day because it would put her to sleep. But he knew little else about who C. J. Lawson was.

"Several packages have been delivered to your suite, Mr. Baron." The young man at reception informed him as he handed over the card key.

"Thank you, Jason." Chase made it a point to refer to the people who worked for him or did business with him by name. Unlike most companies whose CEOs only considered the bottom line, Chase ran the company the same way his grandfather had, with an iron fist, but the safety and morale of his employees always came first. The last time Chase had checked into the resort for a cousin's birthday celebration, Jason and he had held a lengthy conversation over the effects of the current economy on the hotel and travel trades. For a young man at the start of his career, the guy had a good head on his shoulders.

Despite Chase's assurance to C.J. that the accommodations would be plenty spacious and with no strings attached, he could feel the waves of tension emanating from her. She stood nearby in that same rigid stance he'd grown accustomed to seeing. He'd even begun to tense up himself. "Our suites are in the building across the path. If you don't mind, it's a very short walk, or I could have them bring around a golf cart."

"I'd prefer to walk. Normally I run in the morning, and I haven't been able to the last few days."

Chase waved her through the rear double doors and the path to their accommodations. "Kyle raves about running on the beach here. It's very quiet and very private. If you'd like, we can do an early morning run tomorrow."

"That would be nice. Is six too early?"

"The sun doesn't rise until almost seven."

"I know. I like to watch it come over the horizon."

"Then six o'clock it is." From where they stood, he could see the row of outer buildings dotted along the beachfront perimeter of the resort. "We're in the first suite as you reach the building. The Governor and Grams are next door. Mitch and Craig are in the two in the next building, then Eve is in the one-bedroom suite overlooking the gardens."

"You mentioned other family. Who else will be coming?"

"The bets are still out on whether or not my father will show up. He and my grandfather are having a bit of a snit over Father's wife number four. My mother is due to arrive Thursday evening. This will be the first Baron family shindig she'll have attended since … well, for a long time. As for the rest of the Barons, my father is one of six children, and this is the first wedding since Mitch's, so there should be a good-size crowd, except for my uncle Jim, the eldest, who was killed in a training accident during the first Gulf War."

"I'm sorry for your loss."

"Thank you. I was too young to remember him, but his two sons will be here."

"Not their wives?"

"They're not married."

"Oh."

"That's one of the Governor's complaints. Most of his grandchildren circle about on either side of thirty, and yet none are married."

"Really? Out of how many cousins?"

"I have twenty-one first cousins, four siblings, and two half sisters. Paige is from wife number two, while Dad was still married to my mother—"

"Oh, dear. That sounds messy."

"It was. My grandfather was less than happy. I don't think my mother has ever fully recovered. But the affair apparently lasted much longer than the marriage did. Paige is on a business trip she couldn't get out of, but she'll be here in time for the nuptials. My other half sister"—he felt his cheeks tug at the edges of his mouth—"Siobhan. Her mom's Irish. Maura fell for Dad's charms and got pregnant before she figured out Dad didn't have a clue how to be a faithful husband. Siobhan is pretty cool. She's barely out of college, but she's got lots of spunk. She's all Baron with an Irish twist."

"You really like her."

"I really *love* her. Family is important to Barons—no matter how connected or how much of an idiot the father is. It's why the Governor has become so crazy about finding everyone spouses."

"And why you felt the need to bring a date."

"More like a distraction. A little bit of smoke and mirrors. I'm hoping, if he thinks I'm seeing someone, he'll focus on any of my other siblings or cousins."

"And how many of these cousins are attending?"

"Frankly I lost count, but I think it will be near a full house. Every time we have a birth or baptism, the event becomes a borderline circus of Barons."

"Baptisms? I thought you said all the cousins were single and teetering on thirty?"

"I did. A few of the younger aunts and uncles got married a little older and have younger kids, and, of course, both my half sisters are quite a few years younger than the rest of us. I remember their baptisms very well. I think the Governor went especially hog wild on those to make sure everyone understood the girls were as much a Baron as my mom's kids."

"Did any of your other aunts or uncles have second families?"

He nodded. "My uncle Doug has two kids in their late teens, but my aunt Margie passed away from cancer. For a while there he came pretty darn close to crawling into a grave beside his wife."

"But then he met his current wife?"

Chase nodded. "My aunt Eileen was my cousin Adam's math teacher. Adam really stank at math, so he constantly goofed off in class."

"And your uncle constantly met with the teacher." C.J. smiled. A sweet smile that made him want to smile back.

"They were married as soon as the school year ended. And, just in case you're curious, Adam's an actuary."

C.J.'s sparkling brown eyes rounded like chocolate coins. "I thought he stank at math."

"So did everyone else. We're not sure if he started *getting* math because his stepmom was a math teacher who made him pay attention or—"

"If he stank at math so his teacher would become his stepmom."

Chase nodded. "Yeah."

"So basically what you're saying is, with this many grandchildren in attendance, I don't have to worry about being interrogated by your grandparents?"

"Absolutely." At least that was his plan.

CHAPTER EIGHT

Now C.J. understood why Kyle hurried to book the suites early. Propped against a tiny sandy hillside, at least a hill by Texas standards, the detached dwellings might have fit in with the resort's modern architecture, but, to her, they looked like they belonged on any vineyard in Tuscany. Their suite touted three bedrooms, two living areas, a study, a laundry room, a full kitchen—though she couldn't imagine anyone who could afford to stay here would take the time to do their own cooking—gleaming hardwood floors, and a killer view of the ocean. The three-quarter wraparound balcony called to her.

"Housekeeping put you in the master bedroom." Chase stood behind her at the edge of the expansive living room.

She could see from his reflection in the glass that he'd been watching her. Even when not meeting head-on but deflected by a shiny piece of glass, knowing his eyes were on her sent tiny bursts of sparkly tingles up her spine. *Only business*, she reminded herself and her traitorous tingles. "I don't need the master."

Leaning against the wall, ankles crossed, and looking amazing with his crisp white shirt rolled up at his forearms and his sunglasses perched atop his head, allowing her to soak in his steel blue eyes, Chase shrugged. "The secondary bedrooms aren't a hardship."

C.J. spun about, glancing left and right, then up the stairs. Two story suites. Who knew?

"All bedrooms are upstairs. Master's at the end of the hall. Your clothes are already unpacked and put away."

"Someone put away my things?"

"Not someone. The maid."

"Since when do hotel maids unpack for the guests?"

"Since the resort CEO decided to offer luxury suite guests the use of a private maid and cook if requested. The Governor always requests the personalized service."

And why didn't that surprise her? For a guy who retired as a lieutenant colonel, Chase's grandfather sure behaved an awful lot like a five-star general accustomed to having the tiniest detail of his day handled by other people. Of course a great deal of his grandfather's behavior probably came more from the Baron money and his time in the governor's mansion than his years in the military. Maybe.

Turning slowly, she paused to look head on at Chase. Sometimes she wished she could be more spontaneous, like her sister. Maybe then she could throw out the rule book and renegotiate their *business*. When she'd first considered her sister's odd acting job here as performing for some rich old lecher, making it clear that there would be no intimate benefits seemed critically important. Even when she'd first met Chase and discovered, instead of old, he was rather easy on the eyes, she still felt the need to protect herself against the lecher factor. Now, staring at Chase Baron—handsome, smart, considerate, and, yes, charming—she concluded that negotiations were highly overrated. "I'll check out the rooms."

Chase didn't move, didn't speak, only nodded.

Upstairs she made her way down the hall and peeked into each of the bedrooms. The first one was of average size and in light and breezy shades. The next one, a little larger, had a set of keys and a man's wallet on the night table. Chase's. He must have emptied his pockets earlier when he'd gone upstairs to check on her delivery. The master was by far the biggest room. Even bigger than she'd expected and, of course, with a king-size bed. A bed intended to be used by two people. Which matched the enormous Jacuzzi in the bathroom, also intended for two. The oversize shower, on the other hand, was large enough for a small cocktail party.

Most of her adult life she'd lived on base; it was easier and cheaper. Deployed, well, she was lucky. As a female officer she could expect a tent with a half a dozen or less fellow officers instead of the fifty or more Marines crammed into a human oven. But at no point in her life had she ever set foot in luxury anywhere close to this. Talk about living in two different worlds. Until today she didn't realize just how much "the haves" had compared to "the have nots."

"I hope you find the room satisfactory." A young woman with a slight accent smiled up at her. "I'm Rosa, the maid. If you need anything, dial nine to call me. My room is off the kitchen so you have much privacy."

"Thank you. I'm sure I'll be fine." She wouldn't have the first clue what to ask a maid to do for her.

"Very well. Mr. Baron has asked for lemonade on the terrace. I will go now and take care of that."

C.J. bobbed her head. Lemonade on the terrace. She had a feeling the lemonade wasn't made with crystals from a packet, but that Rosa would be downstairs squeezing lemons the old-fashioned way.

"Any problems?" This time the voice in the doorway belonged to Chase.

"No. It's fine, but I still don't need the master."

"We won't be here very much anyhow. I've asked Rosa to serve lemonade on the terrace, but I'm afraid I have to head to the *Baroness*. Need my laptop. Once I take care of a few details, I'll be back with my things. Will you be all right on your own?"

"Of course." She'd been taking care of herself and everyone around her for a heck of a long time; she could certainly handle herself for one afternoon. Even if she did feel like a bull in a china shop.

"If you want company, Eve has already moved into her suite. My brothers are off playing tennis with a friend of Kyle's, but they should all be moving onto the property soon."

"Sounds good." She nodded.

He bobbed his head back at her, but neither made a move. She thought for a second his attention had darted over her shoulder to the bed behind her, but he blinked and instead focused on her. "Well"—he cleared his throat, his gaze lingering on hers—"I should get going."

All she could do was nod again. How ridiculous was it that she didn't want him to leave. She'd known this man less than twenty-four hours and, in the grand scheme of things, knew next to nothing about him, and yet a part of her already missed him.

Tapping his hand on the door jamb, he took a step back. "I won't be long."

She opted not to follow him out of the room. Instead she waited until she heard the door downstairs click shut and wondered what the heck was happening to her?

The call from Chase's office had caught him off guard. Eve was right; the last few years he'd eased away from social responsibilities, leaving any representation of the Baron name at galas, charities, and fund-raisers to his siblings. Instead he tied himself to board meetings, factory inspections, OSHA committees, and the occasional golf game if it meant closing another deal. Except the last two days he'd been so wrapped up bringing C.J. into his world, he'd forgotten about today's scheduled videoconferences.

"Hey, bro." Kyle waved from a side path. "Where you off to in such a hurry?"

"Back to the *Baroness*. Have a videoconference with the chief engineers at the new Honolulu project." He flipped his wrist. "Ten minutes ago."

"I've got an office set up on the other side of the tennis courts. You can take your call there if you prefer." Kyle waved a thumb over his shoulder, then turned to his brothers and friend. "You guys don't mind taking a short detour? Or you can start the game without me."

Jack Preston shrugged. "Nah, I can wait a few minutes to beat your pants off."

"In your dreams," Kyle shot back.

Shaking his head, Jack turned to Chase. "Your brother is delusional."

"So I've been told." He laughed, falling in step next to one of Kyle's best friends. "I hear you're escorting Eve to the wedding."

"Affirmative." Jack kept his gaze forward.

Chase didn't know what to make of that. Was the guy just watching where he was going or avoiding looking him in the eye? "So we'll see you at the ranch for the family dinner?"

Jack shook his head. "Can't. Only have time for a little tennis this afternoon, have to head to Dallas for a few days. I'll be making it back to Galveston the afternoon of the wedding."

"I still can't believe Andrew is getting married. That's as crazy as the thought of my brother Knockout Kyle– the most eligible bachelor three years running—tying the knot."

Slowing his gate, Jack chuckled under his breath, then lowered his voice for Chase's ears only. "Don't know when or who, but mark my words, whenever Kyle does fall, he's going to fall hard." He flashed a knowing grin at Chase. "All of you are."

Kyle flipped the light switch. "Here you go, bro. Anything you want. Password for the computer is capital N, e, e, d, capital F, o, r, capital S, p, 3, 3 d."

"Got it." His brother's cheesy password, a twist on Need For Speed, told him that Jack was dead wrong about Kyle. His brother was never going to slow down long enough for any woman to catch him. Stepping over to the desk, Chase pulled out the desk chair. "You guys have a good game."

"Will do." Pulling the door shut, Kyle popped his head in at the last second. "And I know your date is just temporary, but take some advice from the smarter brother."

"Smarter. Right." Chase shook his head and took a seat in front of the computer.

Kyle rolled his eyes. "She's not what any of us expected from your description. You may want to rethink your choices. Another Baron wedding wouldn't be so awful. As long as it's not me of course."

"Don't do me any favors." His brother closed the door behind him and Chase focused on the screen in front of him. Too bad, all he could think of was CJ all fired up over a cup of coffee, and then spinning in purple swirl. Suddenly his week was looking to be much longer, and more dangerous than he'd thought. Just what he didn't need.

CHAPTER NINE

Walking along the shoreline, C.J. had to admit that whoever designed the Gulf Coast Resort and Golf Club certainly had the concept of comfort and luxury down pat. Add the backdrop of the Galveston shoreline and she was hard-pressed to think of a better place to decompress. So why was she still feeling wound tighter than a steel guitar string?

"There you are."

The unexpected male voice so close startled her. Instinctively she spun about to plant her elbow in somebody's solar plexus, grabbing hold of an arm, she caught a glimpse of Chase's face before fully executing her move. She hadn't expected him to be done with his appointments so quickly. Shifting her weight awkwardly in a last-ditch effort to avoid knocking him on his rear, she stumbled back, her feet sliding out from under her. Blowing out a breath, she braced to land hard on her back, only to feel strong hands slide under her and pull her into a twist of arms and legs before she landed like a lead weight on one Chase Baron.

It took a second for Chase to catch his breath. Staring up at her through slitted eyes, he muttered, "You okay?"

"I was about to ask you that."

"I didn't mean to startle you."

"I didn't mean to take you down either."

Chase blinked up at the sun, sucked in a deep breath,

then lowered his lashes to settle his gaze on her. "What is it that you do for a living anyhow?"

"I'm a nurse." One who didn't need to have studied biology to recognize the perfect alignment of male and female—on a public beach.

"With moves like that, where—the South Bronx?"

"Close." She didn't want to go there. Especially not now. Instead she drew on what little common sense she might still have and shoved up and over, settling beside him on her back, staring up at the blue sky. "I'm sorry."

Chase rolled to his side and, propping himself on one elbow, stared down at her. "Who are you, Cassandra Jane Lawson?"

She didn't get a chance to answer. Before she could even contemplate how to address the question, her mind went utterly and completely blank from the very first second his lips pressed gently against hers. If she was looking for a way to lose herself, and her mind, she'd found it. No hands. No body heat. No physical contact of any kind except the hard and soft pressure of mouth to glorious mouth. And then, just as unexpectedly as he'd started, Chase pulled away, her lips almost trembling from the loss. Heavens, how she wanted to do that again.

Still leaning over her, Chase scanned her face from forehead to chin, pausing briefly at her eyes and again on her mouth. The fire in his eyes as he stared at her still-tingling lips told her that he didn't want to stop any more than she had. "There's been a change in plans for dinner."

Her heart skipped an anxious beat. Were they about to renegotiate their deal?

"Kyle's hosting a small celebration dinner on the *Baroness*"

"Don't they have enough wedding parties planned?"

He still hadn't moved his laser focus from her eyes. Almost like, if he looked at her lips, their evening would be spent right here on the beach—to heck with the general public. "This isn't about the wedding. One of his best friends is having a baby, and Andrew and Nancy missed the big announcement. They want to be part of the good news. I didn't have the heart to say no."

"How many people is a *small* gathering?" Under the circumstances it was a rather ridiculous question, but she wasn't sure she was up to a Baron-caliber performance tonight.

"The expectant parents. Another of their close friends and his wife. And of course my siblings. I don't think Eve is bringing her date."

C.J. did the math in her head. She already knew the siblings. Maybe tonight wouldn't be much of a big deal.

Chase shoved to his knees and pushed to his feet, extending his hand to her. Almost afraid of the contact, she wove her fingers with his, sprang upward, and practically slammed into his chest. Standing so close together in the setting sun, they cast a single silhouette on the sand.

Shaking his head, he broke his hold on her. "We need to dust this sand off and head to Kyle's."

She nodded her agreement, torn between needing to clear her mind to figure out what the heck was going on and dumping all common sense to hash out new terms right this very minute. But she wasn't like her sister. This was a business arrangement. Rules and working in good order was how she lived her life. She would not toss aside all good sense over one kiss. "We'd better get this show on the road." As long as they could perform their roles more than ten feet apart from each other, everything would be just fine. And, if she believed that, maybe it was time to start selling beachfront property in Vegas.

Somewhere in the back of her mind the words *yacht* and *luxury* went side by side but never had she expected to walk aboard the *Baroness* and find it as big and opulent as the *Titanic*. The boat even came with its own helicopter. Every place Chase took her was more extravagant than the one before. Creamy leather and brightly polished wood or marble covered every surface, depending on whether it was meant for sitting, standing, or serving on. C.J. really hoped her eyes weren't bugging out of her head. This was so *not* her world. From the second she and Chase had stepped from the car and she looked across the way to where the boat was anchored, she couldn't think of a thing to say. Over a hundred feet long and four floors high, the thing really did feel as big as the *Titanic*. Heck, the cabin cruiser used to transport them to the real boat was bigger than most apartments she'd lived in. Now standing at the bar in the upper deck lounge, she had yet to sit on the pretty leather furniture. She felt much too much like an interloper.

"In honor of the mom-to-be, we've got apple cider or ginger ale." Bartending, Chase's brother Kyle waved his hands across an array of different bottles and glasses to choose from.

"Ginger ale, please." She hesitantly accepted the glass. Not ordinary glass. Etched crystal. On a boat. How much money did these people have? "Thank you."

Kyle glanced around, spotting Chase and his other brothers huddled at the opposite side of the surprisingly large lounge. "How you holding up so far?"

"Fine. Thank you." She lied. With a bunch of rebel-rousing Marines she could fit in, but, in this world, making a stupid blunder was way too likely.

"You look like you have something to say and no one to say it to."

Interesting observation. She certainly wouldn't tell the owner of this vessel that it was big enough to transport a battalion of Marines. "Your boat is lovely."

He spat out a muffled chuckle. "Well at least one woman in this entourage thinks so. Andrew's new bride-to-be had no problem letting me know she hates it. Says it looks like the *Titanic*."

This time C.J. had to swallow a laugh. If she thought she'd liked Nancy before, she really liked her now. "It is rather … impressive."

"That's not the way Nancy describes it. Good thing it's not Andrew's boat or before their vows were finished she'd be doing a little redecorating."

"People actually redecorate boats?"

"Sure. A home away from home, but no one will be redecorating this baby any time soon. I happen to like it just the way it is."

"There is plenty of… leather."

"Best for dealing with water and humidity. Throw one party where everyone comes in with wet swimsuits and towels on fabric, and, the next thing you know, your yacht smells like a wet dog. Not optimal."

Looking around at all the people, C.J. noted every last one was dressed in casual clothes that she now knew from experience probably cost more than the monthly budget for some small cities. Even dressed up like one of them, she still felt like a mule in a thoroughbred stable. "I don't understand why you need something so big."

The tips of his ears actually turned a dark pink. "In my line of work, there are a lot of parties. This boat has been everywhere from Monte Carlo to Boston. If a party was big enough, we'd be there. Sometimes I'd start my own."

"You poaching your brother's girl?" Empty glass in hand, Andrew teased his cousin, then glanced up just as his fiancée put her hand on a woman's tummy across the room.

C.J. was taken aback by the sheer adoration in his eyes. Andrew had all the charm of every Baron she'd met so far, but she'd gladly sign up for long term duty with a much less handsome and charming guy if he looked at her that same way. And then, as though by silent communication, Nancy glanced up, locked gazes with Andrew, and quickly made her way over.

Nancy soon-to-be Baron sidled up to her fiancé. "Doesn't she look radiant?"

"Absolutely. Too bad she can't hold a candle to you."

"Oh"—Nancy smacked Andrew playfully—"Suck up. You do know that I'm a sure thing?"

C.J. swallowed a lungful of ginger ale.

Nancy gave her fiancé a peck on the cheek. "Go talk man stuff with your friends. I'll entertain C.J."

Andrew planted a tender kiss on her cheek and smacking his cousin on the shoulder, muttered, "I don't think we're wanted here," and the two cousins wandered over to where his brothers and friends stood.

"How are you holding up with the Barons?"

C.J. resisted the urge to find a mirror and see what she looked like that caused everyone to ask her the same question. Did it show that she was a down-to-earth military gal, totally out of her element? "So far so good."

"Don't let them intimidate you." Immediately she raised her hand to stop C.J. from saying anything. "Not that I mean they're bullies or anything, but rich and powerful families have a force field all their own, and some people have a harder time than others functioning around them."

"They are an impressive bunch." No way would C.J. admit that this family get-together scared the dickens out of her. She wasn't an actress like her sister. Standing in the middle of all this luxury, she had no idea what had possessed her to think she could make anyone believe Chase Baron would pick a girl like her to be with. Maybe if it were a picnic in a park—though, knowing these people, there'd be linen tablecloths, sterling silverware, and chefs in white hats regardless.

"They're a good bunch. The Governor was rather gruff to me at first, but, once he realized that I'm not after the money, he was a changed man, well, let's just say he warmed up a bit."

"Military men aren't known for being warm and fuzzy, especially not lieutenant colonels."

"You're familiar with the Marines?"

C.J. nodded. "Used to be."

Nancy eyed her carefully. "The trick is to remember, under all the trappings, they're the same as you and me. Flesh and blood with hopes and dreams." Her gaze shifted to Mitch. "And sorrows."

"He loved his wife very much, didn't he?"

"I don't know firsthand, but it sure looks that way to me. Andrew says, at first, Mitch seemed to be in a permanent fog. He hasn't fully come out of it, but he appears to be a little better. I keep hoping that, hanging around here, the resort's motto will rub off on him."

"Motto?"

"*Come to Gulf Shores, kick off your shoes, and fall in love*. From what I understand, some marketing guru came up with it. I suspect Mitch's problem is he hasn't kicked his shoes off."

"Thanks for the warning. I'll remember to keep mine on."

Again Nancy carefully eyed C.J., then let her glance drift over to Chase and back. "I don't know about that."

C.J. stole a peek at Chase over the rim of her glass. She knew. Kicking off her shoes where Chase Baron was involved would be a huge mistake. Oil and water never mix.

CHAPTER TEN

All evening Chase got the distinct impression that C.J. was avoiding him. At first she seemed stiff and distant. Nervous perhaps. Or just observing. He honestly couldn't tell with her. By the time dinner was served buffet-style on the sundeck, she'd made friends with the other women and seemed to be having a more relaxed time. He'd even caught her chatting up a bit with his brother Mitch. At first he hadn't thought anything of it. Mitch was a politician; he could make nice with anyone. Good at kissing babies and all that sort of thing.

Not until Chase had spotted them in deep conversation over dessert did he get an uneasy feeling in his gut, and, when he tried to step into the conversation, C.J. excused herself, saying she needed to use the ladies' room. The way Mitch casually kept an eye on her as she walked away had Chase's gut doing backflips.

"You two seemed to be hitting it off." Chase made an effort at nonchalance. Normally in business that came easily. Part of that *never let them see you sweat* thing. But, in his personal life, and with this brother, he wasn't sure he could pull it off.

"Hey," Mitch responded, "any woman who wants to talk politics has my undivided attention."

"You were talking politics?"

His brother nodded. "She has some pretty grounded opinions on the military and the US role in the Middle East.

Has some interesting facts too." His eyes narrowed in thought. "The Governor is going to like her."

"The Governor hopefully won't get much chance to chat with her. And you'd better find someone to bring along to these events, or you may find yourself on the short end of his matchmaking stick."

Mitch shook his head. "No, not me. He's got his eyes set on the single guys."

Chase stopped himself before he blurted out the painful reminder that Mitch was indeed single. Instead he forced a smile. "We'll have to see about that."

A cool breeze on the bay had the party lingering on the deck instead of moving to the air-conditioned interior. Occasionally Chase heard laughter from the women, among talk of babies and bridesmaids' dresses and cake-tasting. The guys talked mostly sports with the occasional diversion to Wall Street and the upcoming elections. But it wasn't until the party was breaking up that Chase spotted Mitch and C.J. once again huddled together, ginger ale flutes in hand.

Only this time C.J.'s laughter made the uneasy feeling in his gut ride up his spine and settle tensely in his jaw. He didn't need one hand to count how often in private he'd seen Mitch smile the last couple of years, and tonight—for the first time in a long while—that smile reached his eyes. And that just made Chase grind down even harder on his back teeth. He didn't like it one little bit. He'd found C.J. first.

Taking a calming breath, he closed his eyes. Their business arrangement had brought her here in the first place. Of course it was only natural for him to feel protective of her. Even from his brother. As for the kiss, after she'd taken him down like a judo expert, practically lying on top of her, the kiss was a natural reaction. It didn't mean anything. Basic human chemistry. That had to be all it was.

Crossing the short distance between them, Chase stood over the corner seating area where Mitch and C.J. were chuckling. "Looks like it's time to call it a night."

"Oh." C.J. flipped her wrist. "I didn't realize how late it is."

"You know what they say." Mitch shrugged. "Time flies when you're having fun."

Her shoulders relaxed, and she angled her head. "Yes. Yes, it does."

Kyle's words the other day sprang to mind. *She's not what any of us expected from your description. You may want to rethink your choices. Another Baron wedding wouldn't be so awful.* His brother had been right about at least one thing, CJ was turning out to be more than anyone expected. Before Chase could shout something stupid like "She's mine" or worse "Buy your own date," he took a short step back and extended his hand. "Shall we?"

C.J. nodded, stood, but didn't take his hand. "It was nice chatting."

"Yes, it was." Mitch extended his hand, and Chase bit down on his back teeth again when she accepted and shook it.

"I guess I'll see you at dinner tomorrow," she said softly.

"And, remember," Mitch continued to smile, "the Governor is mostly all bark nowadays."

"I'll keep that in mind." She dipped her chin and turned on her heel.

Chase spit out a neutral "Night" to his brother and spun away after C.J., without saying anything he couldn't later take back. Or doing something he could get thrown in jail for.

★

What she had been dreading all night loomed over her like the Tower of London in the days of executions. No matter how many thousands of square feet or how many bedrooms the suite had, none of it felt big enough for the two of them.

Swallowing hard, she spoke few words, with the exception of the benign occasional comment about the party or the pleasant weather, during their short trip back to the suite. A heavy feeling of apprehension settled over her with the blanket of evening fog.

"Here we go." Chase slid the key card into the lock and shoved open the door.

Without all the bright sunlight, the previously large space felt considerably more confining. And intimate.

"Well ..." C.J. dropped her purse on the nearby easy chair and looked at the stairs.

"Would you like something to drink? Tea, coffee?"

Yes, something to wrap her hands around besides him. "Too late for coffee, but tea would be nice. I'll make some."

"No need. The maid has probably been bored all day, waiting for something to do."

"You're going to bother her now?"

Chase glanced at his watch and shrugged. "It's only eleven o'clock."

"No." C.J. pushed ahead. "I can zap a mug in the microwave as well as the next guy."

For a second Chase seemed startled by her response but hefted another lazy shoulder. "Works for me."

In the kitchen she checked a few cupboards, looking for cups.

Chase opened a drawer for spoons and napkins. "You and Mitch seemed to hit it off."

"He's a nice guy. So is Kyle. I didn't get much chance to visit with Craig."

From another cupboard, Chase pulled out saucers for under the mugs. "You like talking politics?"

"Not really." Truth was, she'd felt horribly sorry for Mitch. When his guard was down, his eyes held a sadness that any stranger could see. "He loved his wife a lot, didn't he?"

Chase sucked in a big breath. "Yeah. They'd been college sweethearts. Abie was something else. Smart, sassy, and could keep all the Barons in line. Even the Governor."

"I bet. I could tell from the way he spoke about her."

Setting the silverware on the table with a clank, Chase spun about. "He talked about Abie?"

C.J. nodded her head.

"He never talks about her. I mean, her name might get mentioned on occasion, but he never *talks* about her."

"Oh." C.J. pulled the hot mugs out of the microwave. "Maybe if he talked about her more, it would make moving on easier for him."

"I don't know. None of us do. Even the Governor treads lightly around him, and treading lightly is not the Governor's way."

"So I've heard." Leaning back against the counter, C.J. blew into her tea. "The ladies were very friendly too. I thought they were teasing me when they told me Nancy makes soaps."

"Don't laugh. That soap business of hers does very well."

"That's what she said. The perfect combination of business savvy with natural and organic and of course the trump card, made in the USA." C.J. took a cautious sip. The hot brew burned the tip of her tongue, but she swallowed anyhow. Better her tongue than other places that were already steaming up. "I think I'll call it a night."

"Yeah. Sure." Chase set his untouched mug on the table and followed her up the stairs.

How was it that he climbed more than a step behind her and yet she could feel the heat of his body as sharply as though he were pressed up against her? And wasn't that someplace she didn't need her mind to go. Refusing to look back, knowing that, if she saw him, her military resolve might shatter, she didn't speak until she reached her bedroom door. "Good night."

Softly, from his door, Chase's voice crossed the distance, lower and huskier than usual. "Night."

Twenty-four hours with Chase and already this charade was wearing thin. How was she supposed to get through the rest of the week?

CHAPTER ELEVEN

Only six o'clock in the morning and Chase was more than ready for another cold shower. He'd taken a long one last night. Not that it had helped him sleep any easier. When he got back to Dallas, he should get his head out of the office and spend a little more time with female companionship. How sad was it that an employee, so to speak, had him all bent out of shape? For now, a long run on the beach might help work out some of the frustration.

The only problem with that plan was C.J. herself. Waiting for him downstairs, even in a pair of maroon running shorts and an oversized khaki T-shirt, she looked as stunning as in the purple gown.

Short boyish hair, no makeup, and a shirt big enough for a sumo wrestler should not have looked so blasted good on her at the near crack of dawn. Neither did it help that C.J. had gorgeous legs that seemed to run all the way to her neck. This was a woman who definitely knew physical activity. He'd always thought himself a boob man. In that oversized T-shirt, it was impossible to tell if C.J. even had boobs, but dang did she have legs. Shapely, toned, strong, and, if he didn't start thinking of something extremely unpleasant, like Chinese water torture, he'd find himself going down a dangerous path. "Ready?"

"More than."

She had the door open and was trotting down the path before he'd taken his first step. It took a few minutes to find a rhythm that worked for both of them. He wasn't in the habit of jogging on the beach, and, until he moved to C.J.'s opposite side on the more packed sand, he'd struggled just a little. Not that he would ever admit that.

The way C.J. kept a steady pace, he could tell running was definitely a regular routine for her. The sun crept over the horizon, changing the dull gray to strings of blue and pink and finally burning yellow over the water with the strewn clouds taking on colorful hues.

"I love the sunrise." C.J. slowed her pace.

"What about sunset?"

"That too, but there's something about the promise of a new day, a new beginning, that offers me more peace."

"Are you looking for peace, C.J.?"

Her gaze in the distance, she eased out of a trot to a gentle walk. "I suppose I am. What about you?"

"Me?" He shortened his stride to keep in step with her. "My life is very peaceful."

"I guess that's why you have to hire dates for family events?"

"That would be *date*. As in singular. And that's because my life is complicated, not unpeaceful."

C.J. nodded. "Got it."

"All right." He paused and stretched at the waist, left then right. "Maybe, just maybe, I do envy Andrew a little."

"Ah." C.J. glanced at him sideways, squinting one eye.

"Andrew, like Kyle, always played hard. The stereotypical party boy. Most eligible bachelor. Pick an adjective. He's been called them all. Yet he lived a life that most men dream of. He should have, by all rights, been the happiest guy around."

"But he wasn't," C.J. stated rather than asked.

"I don't know that deep down any of us are." The admission surprised him. He'd been thinking that more and more recently, but hearing his own voice say it out loud was startling. He'd convinced himself that running Baron Enterprises was all the fulfillment he needed. Somewhere in the back of his mind he'd always known that "things" couldn't replace emotional stability. His mother had been a living, breathing example that money and power couldn't buy peace and happiness. And yet money and power seemed to be the only thing the women he'd dated had been truly interested in. Not till Mitch and Abie had Chase seen true love in action, and just one brother finding true love Chase could easily write off as a fluke. A once-in-a-blue-moon stroke of luck. Except now another of his generation had hit the jackpot. Slippery odds.

"I wish I could say you were being cynical." C.J. looked around. "I think we left the resort in the dust. If we're going to hoof it back, I need fuel."

Chase scanned the street up the hill. "There's a wonderful little bistro not far from here that serves the best brioche—"

"I have a better idea." Her eyes took on a bright sparkle, and she took off at a slow trot.

Chase fell into step beside her. "Where are we going?"

"There."

She pointed toward the street in the distance, but, between the beach and the park ahead, no structure looked to be a restaurant. "I don't see anything."

"That's because you're not looking."

Of course he was looking. He strained his perfect 20/20 vision looking.

At the concrete curb, she slowed her pace. "These trucks always have the best food."

Truck? Sure enough, she walked right up to a large silver truck with a raised window cut out of the side. "You do realize those things are probably germ factories. Chez Moi is not far from here."

"Nonsense. Closest thing to a mouthwatering greasy

spoon. I've been taking a crash course in your world for almost two days. The least you can do is share a food-truck breakfast with me."

And food poisoning. "Lead the way."

He had no idea why anyone went jogging with money, but C.J. had a small plastic case on a string around her neck with cash, credit card, and driver's license. Who the heck needed a driver's license to run on the beach? But he couldn't fault her efficiency. She'd ordered him a breakfast burrito with the works. He wasn't even sure how much *works* could be in a breakfast wrap.

While he held the two ginormous aluminum-clad bundles, C.J. paid the man for their breakfast and two OJs. Juggling the wraps and drinks, he shrugged. "Sorry I don't jog with cash." Or credit. With the Baron name a mere signature at the best places in any town was enough to guarantee payment.

"Fortunately I do." She took an orange juice from his hand and one wrapped burrito. "Come on. Breakfast will be more pleasant under one of the shade trees in the park."

Curious to see what all was in his steroid-size breakfast, Chase resisted the temptation to peek under the foil and instead distracted himself by watching C.J.'s cute posterior strut across the street to the park.

"Here's a good spot." C.J. plopped heavily onto the garden bench and immediately unwrapped one end of her breakfast.

The large tree she picked looked the same to him as the three other large trees they'd passed en route to this location. "I thought the previous tree was a good spot."

"That's because you haven't taken the time to really look around." Gripping the massive burrito in two hands, poised to take a bite, she looked up through her lashes at him. "First, this tree has wider branches. The sun won't encroach on our space before we're done eating. Second, the bench at the other tree is missing a slat. Third, from here, we can see the playground. There's no better way to brighten a day than when a child laughs with sheer delight at the most ordinary of things. It's really too early for moms and their kids to come around, but, by my sister's place sometimes, a mom or two will show up just to keep the kids busy. They might here as well."

Not sure what to say, he nodded and took a quick look around. She was right about the slats and the shade, but he had no idea about the children. There weren't a whole lot of them running about Baron Industries or the family gatherings—a reason why his grandfather was on a matchmaking tirade.

C.J. took a bite and moaned with delight. Chase on the other hand nearly groaned.

Wrinkling her nose at him, she swallowed another big bite. "So what do you think?"

Before he could fully bite down, his taste buds already understood what C.J. knew. "I have no idea what else is in here besides eggs and potato and maybe some bacon, but wow, this is really good."

"Told ya."

This was the best egg and potato and bacon and who-knew-what-else concoction he'd ever had. He practically inhaled the darn thing it was so delicious.

She took her last bite, crumpled the foil into a ball, and tossed it into a nearby trash can.

No children had come by. Hardly a surprise so early on a Sunday morning. He wished they had though. Something told him he would have enjoyed seeing C.J.'s face as she watched the small children scurrying about. Had the baby news celebration last night reminded her of that ever-ticking biological clock? Or did she always sit in the park and watch the children play? It certainly sounded like she might.

"When was the last time you were on a swing?" C.J. asked.

"I'm not sure I was ever on a swing. My mother wasn't the sort to take me to the park for a playdate."

"Now that's just a crime against human nature. All children should play on swings." She reached out and tugged on the tail of his T-shirt. "Come on."

For the entire length of the short walk, C.J. didn't bother to let go of Chase's shirt. The next thing he knew, he was on the tallest swing on the set, and C.J. was showing him how to pump his legs. "Higher," she screamed. Soon they were both on swings, flying back and forth, up higher than the top. When they pendulumed back in the opposite direction, C.J. leaned backward and squealed.

There was no stopping the smile on his face. He wasn't sure which was more exhilarating, soaring back and forth on the set or watching the smile bloom on C.J.'s face as she flew higher. More than a time or two, he wondered if the strong metal set wouldn't pop up from the ground and take them with it.

"Mommy, look. Like you and Daddy." A little girl, not even tall enough to reach Chase's waist, came running up to the swings and gave him a huge toothy grin. "My daddy pushes my mommy on the swing sometimes, and it makes her laugh. Can you push me?"

"Carolyn," the mom called, hurrying to catch up with her daughter. A single gesture, had had the little girl retreating to her mother's side. Holding hands and moving at a slower pace, by the time mother and child had reached the swing set, both he and C.J. had relinquished their seats.

"I didn't mean to interrupt you." The mom relinquished her hold on the little girl and rested her hands atop her protruding stomach. "I can't keep up with her most of the times. I'm sorry if she bothered you."

"Nonsense." Chase smiled at the woman. "But a gentleman never refuses a lady's request."

The mom stared at him blankly until little Carolyn

grinned up at him again, and, when he nodded, she scurried over to the lowest swing seat and waited for him to give her a little nudge. Pretty soon she was swinging her feet back and forth and, like C.J., calling to go higher. Unfortunately, off to the side, her mother shook her head at him. Little Carolyn would have to wait until she got older to go higher. Just then another little girl ran up to Carolyn, and he and the swing were both forgotten as the two children hurried off to the monkey bars. "Looks like I've been tossed aside," he teased.

"Don't feel bad. Women are known to be fickle." Jogging in place, C.J. tipped her head toward the beach. "We should be getting back now anyhow. You ready?"

"Absolutely. Last one back pushes the other on the swing for a whole month." Chase took off at a quick clip. He was having fun. Real fun. And it wasn't just the swing or the food truck. It was the person who'd introduced him to both. To a softer, simpler side of life. Surprised at C.J.'s ability to keep pace with him, he revved it up a bit. Normally he'd hang back and be the gentleman, give the lady a head start, but suddenly the idea of more time to get to better know the real C. J. Lawson was more important to him than chivalry.

CHAPTER TWELVE

The way things had been explained to CJ, with Andrew and Nancy the only ones likely to add great grandchildren to the family tree any time soon, the aging patriarch seemed to be more willing to spend time in Houston. The Governor probably thought he could talk them into growing the clan sooner than later, but the truth be told, his heart was as deeply rooted in the family ranch. If he had his way, he would probably build a house for every grandchild on their wedding day, but more than an hours drive from the north Houston suburbs, he was doing well to simply have the family join him somewhat regularly for Sunday dinner.

What struck C.J. as ridiculous though, was that she had to pack an overnight bag for dinner. Normal people got dressed in ordinary clothes and took an ordinary leisurely drive to dinner, ate a normal meal, and then returned after dinner to their normal house. Of course there wasn't a single thing about the Baron family that fell under the category of normal *or* ordinary. From what she was told, they would arrive in afternoon-business-casual attire. Lila Baron would most likely serve tea in the late afternoon. The family matriarch didn't have a lick of British heritage, but her dad had been stationed in England for a good many years, and she'd taken a liking to the civility of tea time. So around four o'clock C.J. could expect to sit for tea with the women in the family. At six they would retire to their rooms and change for dinner. Chase had explained that normally attire for Sunday dinners fell into the category of church clothes. Sometimes, if there was work to be done, the family would be seen in jeans and boots, but, for this visit, the Governor had designated the dress as black tie. Dinner would be served promptly at 8:00 p.m., so every member of the family would assemble for cocktails by 7:00 p.m. at the very latest.

"You'd better bring a change of clothes for tomorrow." Chase popped his head into the open doorway to her room. "Dinner will run late, and the Governor will, of course, convince everyone that it's best to stay than drive at night."

C.J. raised a questioning brow.

"I know. He thinks because he can't see at night anymore, neither can the rest of us."

Now it made perfect sense to her that Chase had insisted on purchasing her a full set of luggage to go with her new wardrobe and the matching satin nightgown and robe. Not that anyone should see her in her nightie, but, for all she knew, maids and butlers would be prancing in and out of her room like a modern-day episode of *Downton Abbey*. "Afternoon clothes, dinner clothes, breakfast clothes. Do I need to know anything special about a lunchtime wardrobe change?"

Chase rolled his eyes. "By lunchtime we'll be on the road back to Galveston. The Governor and Grams will move to the resort, and Grams will commence the wedding parties with a formal tea. Or is it the tennis game?"

"Tennis? What the heck does tennis have to do with anything?"

"Barons tend to be a bit competitive. The family will be divvied up in teams and work their way through the day until there's a winner who gets the cup."

"*Cup?*"

"The Baron Cup. Sounds silly but, to a Baron, it might

as well be the Stanley Cup. You'll have to watch out for a few members who tend to cheat a bit. Though that's harder at tennis. Do you play?"

C.J. shook her head. "Only if one summer camp when I was ten counts."

"Probably not. Most likely you'll get paired with one of the stronger players. Eve is actually pretty good. For a while we thought she might go pro."

"Wait a minute. I have to play?" Oh, her sister owed C.J. *big time* for stepping in for her.

A satisfied smile slid across his face. A mischievous sparkle twinkled in his eyes. "Everyone participates."

"But I'm not a Baron."

"You're here with a Baron. That's close enough. At least there's not an obstacle course this time. Grams put her foot down and insisted it wasn't appropriately civilized for a wedding, so the Governor agreed to tennis."

Too bad. *That* she could have done.

Twenty minutes later they were on the road to Sunday dinner. An hour and ten minutes after leaving suburban Houston they were rolling up the winding drive to a massive brick house that reminded her of a civil war plantation. Surprisingly larger than she'd expected and most definitely impressive. "Nice."

"Very different from the modern all glass Baron Tower in Dallas."

"That would definitely have looked out of place in ranch country." The car came to a stop, and Chase hopped out. She was almost a little surprised a valet hadn't popped out of the shrubbery to open the door for her. "Looks like we're the first ones here."

"Why do you say that?"

C.J. waved her arm across the circular drive. "No cars."

"Maybe, but they could be garaged already."

"*Garaged?*"

"Down to the left is a ten-car garage."

Now that it had been pointed out, she did see another building camouflaged by a crop of trees. *Ten-car garage.*

"Mr. Chase." An older man in a suit came out the door, a younger man hurrying around him. "I hope your drive was pleasant."

"Very." Chase smiled. "This is Miss Lawson."

The man, who C.J. guessed had to be the proverbial butler, nodded at her. "Peter here will take care of your belongings. The Governor and Mrs. Baron are receiving family in the parlor."

"Thanks, Jeeves." Chase grabbed hold of her hand and tugged her up the stairs.

"Jeeves? Butlers are really named Jeeves?"

"No. His name is … George, I think. But we've called him Jeeves ever since we were kids. I guess it never occurred to us to call him anything else once we grew up."

"And he doesn't mind?"

"I can't imagine why. We don't say it with any disrespect."

She didn't know what to say, but she had to wonder how George felt about it. Glancing over her shoulder a moment, she saw him giving instructions to the young man who now carried her overnight bag and Chase's garment bag. "Where is he going with our bags?"

Chase paused at the front door and looked past her. "Service entrance."

Before she could digest the idea of a service entrance, she found herself standing in the center hall of a house that looked even larger now than it had from the outside. Slowly she followed Chase across the main foyer and down a few steps into what she could only assume was the parlor. A wall of glass windows looked over an expansive lawn. Though *garden* may have been a more appropriate term. She could also see that, while the front entry was on this level, they were at least one story above the back gardens. If she'd thought the yacht was impressive, she clearly had a lot to learn about the one percent of the population who were truly filthy rich.

The Governor pushed to his feet, and the few men in the room followed. First Chase kissed his grandmother, then shook his grandfather's hand, and one by one made his way around the room, introducing C.J. to anyone she hadn't already met. Every few minutes another Baron arrived, and different levels of cheers and greetings erupted. She could almost guess the family pecking order. She also didn't think there was a single introvert in the bunch. Aside from "How do you do?" and "It's a pleasure to meet you," she hadn't been required to speak much. All the other relatives seemed perfectly happy to carry the conversation. By her count she'd met fourteen cousins, only one of which brought a guest—Emily—to dinner, and, considering that everyone seemed to know her by name, C.J. guessed by the laughter and teasing that Emily had been a part of this family for some while.

"Have you known Chase very long?" Emily asked C.J.

It took C.J. a moment to realize she was being spoken to. "Oh, no. Not terribly long."

Lila Baron sidled up beside Emily. "It's always nice to see you at a family event, dear. The Governor keeps expecting Devlin to smarten up and make you an official Baron."

Emily smiled sweetly at the old woman, but it struck C.J. that there wasn't much longing in her gaze. Maybe Devlin was up to the same tricks as Chase. Only at it longer.

"But C.J."—Lila turned slowly—"I would love to know more about you and my grandson."

"There isn't really much to tell. We haven't known each other that long." Sticking to as much of the truth as possible was the plan, and deflecting whenever she couldn't think of a good lie.

"Well, then tell me something fun. Where did you meet?"

She sucked in a deep breath. *Here we go.* "I was waiting for someone and saw him crossing the restaurant." There. Whew.

"Oh, really?" Lila smiled. "What was the first thing you noticed about my grandson?"

C.J. felt her lips curl at the corners. They hadn't rehearsed this part, but the answer was easy. "That would be his eyes. They're an amazing shade of deep blue."

"Yes. I do believe that's what first drew me to James." It took C.J.'s mind a few moments to process that, to Lila, the Governor would be James. "They drew me in right away, and I guess—as the movie says—he had me at hello."

"That's very sweet," Emily and C.J. echoed.

"Love at first sight always is." Up close, Lila had a softness and a tremendous amount of wisdom and compassion in her gaze that made C.J. very uncomfortable. But the way Lila's last comment seemed to be directed at C.J. had alarm bells in her head sounding and the hairs on the back of her neck rising. Without thinking, C.J. found herself glancing up and scanning the room quickly, relief settling over her as her gaze fell on Chase, chatting with a cousin. Feeling stronger, C.J. returned her attention to the family matriarch only to find the woman's smile had broadened and her eyes, pinned to C.J., twinkled with delight. *Oh, no. What had she done?*

"You'd better go rescue your lady friend." Devlin Baron lifted his chin toward the far corner of the room. "Emily can hold her own in a Baron inquisition but not so sure about your date."

Chase spotted C.J. chatting with his grandmother. He'd done his best to stay at her side, but, whenever the natural flow of conversations separated them, he'd kept one eye on her, ready to swoop in if she needed him. So far she'd done so well that he'd relaxed and gotten distracted, talking business with his favorite cousin. Being the same age, Devlin and Chase were as close as brothers. So much so that Chase had considered letting him in on the C.J. charade but decided, in the end, it was in his best interest to limit insider info to his siblings. And maybe his mother.

When it came to a family hierarchy, no doubt that the Governor ran the roost the same way he'd ridden over his troops in the military. With a strong regimented hand. All the Baron children knew the only reason that strong hand wasn't an iron fist was because of their grandmother, but something in the way Grams gaze twinkled as she stared at C.J. had Chase on high alert. Time to rescue C.J. before the old lady fell for her as much as he had. He couldn't afford for his grandmother to grow too attached. *Too attached.* Too bad he wasn't following his own advice.

He'd made it all of five feet before his cousin Porter cut him off. "I've been chasing you down all evening. Colton and I have been discussing a new project and we want your opinion."

"Oh, good. You found him." Colton came up and stood between Chase and his escape.

Like it or not, rescuing CJ from his grandmother's charms was simply going to have to wait.

CHAPTER THIRTEEN

"It's about time I got my turn." The Governor stood between his wife, now seated, and C.J., still standing with Emily.

"Governor." Emily smiled at the older man, offering a reverent dip of her head.

"Emily." Nothing in the man's voice exuded the friendliness C.J. had noticed during dinner at the resort. And, from the way Emily's eyes dimmed, C.J. was pretty sure she wasn't the only one who had noticed.

"If you'll excuse me"—Emily sidestepped the Governor "I believe Olivia is calling me."

Suddenly, in a room filled with people, C.J. felt very alone. Chase and his siblings had done their best at a game of keep-away, making sure the Governor didn't have the chance to interrogate her, but, at the moment, Chase was in deep conversation with what she assumed were a couple of cousins. She was clearly on her own.

"Why don't you sit down, dear?" Lila waved her husband to the empty chair beside her.

The Governor merely huffed in response. That hadn't surprised C.J. at all. The higher up the ranks the officers climbed, the better they became at intimidation. Standing over a person was top on their list of tools. The other, staring her down, he was using now. She'd stood at attention too many times through the years to be even slightly uncomfortable. Keeping her shoulders straight and her gaze steady on his, she waited for him to make the first move.

"James," Lila said a little louder, breaking the spell.

Chase's grandfather let his gaze drift down to his wife, accompanied by a soft smile. "In a minute." For C.J., the hardness in his eyes had returned. "I understand you're here with my grandson Chase."

"Yes, sir." She still didn't move. She had not been dismissed.

"Do you live here in Texas?"

"Visiting my sister." Though most likely more long term than a typical visit, at least it was the truth.

His gaze remained level with hers. "You believe in family?"

"I would do anything for my sister." C.J. was, after all, here.

"Hmm." He scanned her face, looking for tells.

She recognized the behavior. Had done it herself many a time.

"What about your parents?"

"Father died when I was five. My mother still lives in San Antonio."

"James," Lila spoke up again.

This time retired US Marine and former Governor James Baron Senior hesitated before responding to his wife. His eyes narrowed as he tried to read C.J.'s soul, and then he blew out a soft sigh and dipped his chin. The scrutiny was over; she'd just been dismissed. Able to fully relax, she resisted the urge to clasp her hands behind her back and stand at parade rest.

"I think I'll take that seat now."

For a man with a cane, the old guy moved around very well. C.J. suspected the cane was more a prop than a necessity.

From the corner of her eye, C.J. spotted Chase making a

beeline across the room. The funny part was that Mitch and Eve were also practically sprinting from opposite corners. Foolish people. She'd told them she could hold her own.

"I don't understand." C.J. stood practically glued to the wall. "Why are my bags in here?"

Chase undid his tie and the top button of his collar. "Grams apologized for any inconvenience, but she wasn't expecting Siobhan and her cousin Michael to make it tonight, so Grams put Siobhan in a room with Emily, but there were no more empty beds for Michael so he got your room. Apparently Grams thinks we're … closer than we are."

"Apparently." No way was C.J. moving away from the wall. Even if the bed was king-size. Sharing a room with Chase was not a good idea. Sharing the bed would be insanity.

"What I don't understand is that the Governor has always maintained a strict policy of no ring, no fraternizing."

"Since I don't have a ring—nor do I want one," she added in a rush, "it looks like the rules have changed."

"Hmm."

"Hmm?"

"The Governor doesn't *change*. At least not without a really good reason."

"So what are you saying?"

"My brothers were right."

"About?"

"Bringing you along wouldn't be enough to direct him to the others. It's only succeeded in moving him ahead to scheming for marriage and babies."

"How'd you come to that conclusion?"

Chase arched a knowing brow. "Two people. One bed. Do the math."

"I see what you mean. So now what do we do?" A bevy of famous old movies ran through her head, along with all the shared sleeping-arrangement scenarios. Among the laundry list of solutions fell: sleeping in the bathtub, cramming his six-foot-plus frame into the two easy chairs at the foot of the bed, rigging some kind of makeshift clothesline to hang a blanket between them, or perhaps building a wall of pillows on the bed, and, of course, the old standby—throw the comforter on the floor. None of which were destined to produce a good night's rest for either of them.

Undoing another button, Chase heaved out a heavy sigh. "I need to get out of this monkey suit."

That was not an image she needed him to encourage. "Maybe I can share with Eve?"

Chase stared at the king-size bed and, undoing another button, shook his head. "She's in with our cousin Alice."

"Oh." C.J.'s gaze drifted to his undone shirt and then to the bed. Now she not only had an image of him without his tux on, but without the tux and on the bed. She was in so much trouble.

No matter how many sleeping options ran through Chase's mind, every last one of the possibilities finished with him breaking his promise to her.

Raking his fingers through his hair and leaving his hand hooked around his neck, he reconsidered his options—again. "You take the bed. I'll take the floor." And sleep in his pants. If he kept his pants on, he might pull this off.

"You can't sleep on the floor. You won't get any rest."

At this point, no matter what, rest would not be an option. Sleeping down the hall from her at the suite had been nearly impossible; having her in the same room would be nothing more than guaranteed torture. He could sleep when he returned to Dallas. "It will be fine."

Unbelieving brown eyes studied his.

Only now did he see the concern and trepidation sparring inside her. *Blast.* A different type of need twisted in his gut. Yes, he wanted her, more than he should. Besides a literal aching need to be near her, an even stronger need pushed him to make her feel safe. To take away the doubts and fears he saw battling inside her. To protect her. Here. Now. Always. And wasn't that a startling desire.

Wrapping tensed fingers around his loosened tie, he yanked it from his collar. "You can use the bathroom to change. I'll set up a pallet over by the window."

C.J. nodded and took a tentative step forward. Her bag was open on the luggage rack behind him. "Excuse me." Walking nearly sideways to put as much distance between them as possible, C.J. inched past him.

Why did this massive room feel so small? She'd barely made it to the bathroom without tackling him first only to realize her toothbrush was still in her overnight bag. She really needed to screw her head on straight. He was just a man. She'd lived and worked side by side with hundreds of other men. Some better looking than others. Some nicer than others. So why was Chase Baron posing such a problem for her?

"I seem to have forgotten ..." Holding a tube of toothpaste in one hand, C.J. spun about to return to the bathroom and nearly crashed into him. Her mouth going very dry. "My, uh, toothbrush."

He stood perfectly still.

"I, uh …" C.J. bit her lower lip. Her gaze dropped from his eyes to his mouth, and suddenly she forgot what she was about to say.

"C.J."

Her name sounded hollow and far away, followed by a light tapping sound.

"Chase." His cousin Siobhan's voice carried into the room as the bedroom door squeaked open. "Grandpa says we can go … Oops."

Even though they were innocently standing within each other's breathing space, C.J. sprang back and snapped almost to attention.

"Sorry. I … I'll talk to you—"

"No." Chase sucked in a sharp breath. "What did the Governor say?"

"That the *Fidelis* is being delivered in a few days. Can we take her out?"

He dragged his gaze away from C.J. and turned to face his youngest sister. "I'm sure we can work something out."

Siobhan's face brightened. "Cool! And, um, sorry if I interrupted anything."

C.J. glanced at Chase, and he shook his head at his little sister. "You'd better let Devlin know too."

"On my way!" Siobhan squealed with delight and pulled the door closed behind her.

"I'm sorry—" Chase started.

"Don't." She raised her hand and, with her back to him, rummaged through her bag and spun around, holding one of the satin nightgowns from the shopping day. "I should get ready for bed."

Teeth clean and her full length robe tied snuggly closed, she stared at her reflection in the mirror. This little charade was becoming complicated with a capital *C*. Time to face the firing squad.

Standing at the foot of the bed, already changed into sleeping pants and a t-shirt, Chase yanked the spread off the bed. "It's warm enough that you should be comfortable with just the sheet and blanket."

"I can't let you sleep on the floor." She tossed her change of clothes on a nearby chair. "Your back will complain for a week, and you won't get any sleep."

"It's unlikely I'll get any sleep anyhow."

"Excuse me?" She stood board straight.

"That didn't come out right. What I meant was, it'll be hard, literally, for me to fall asleep."

Why did men need to be so macho? "All the more reason I should take the floor and you the bed."

"Not happening." He shook his head with purpose.

Great macho and stubborn. "I've had a lot more practice sleeping on the ground than you have."

He let loose a muffled chuckle.

"You don't believe me?" Macho, stubborn, and mocking her. Anger and frustration tumbled over each other. She crossed her arms and good sense flew out the window as she opened her mouth. "When my unit first arrived in Afghanistan, there'd been a few ... complications. I spent the better part of a week on the hard ground in full uniform in an oven disguised as a tent."

"Afghanistan?" Incredulity dripped with every syllable.

C.J. tapped her foot. "Yes, Afghanistan."

"What were you doing there?"

"I told you. I'm a nurse."

"From the South Bronx," he mumbled and then his back stiffened. "Wait. You're in the military?"

"Was."

"Between jobs," he quietly repeated her earlier words to him.

The euphemism she'd used for a person who had been fired or downsized had come back to bite her.

"We need to talk." He turned on his heel and strode toward the door.

"Where are you going?"

"To find you something more practical to change into, and then we'll both get on that bed and talk."

Her jaw dropped open and then snapped shut as she bit down hard on her back teeth. Why was she blessed with such a big mouth?

Standing in the open doorway, he paused to face her, a strong, and yes stubborn, glint in his eyes. "I said talk."

Maybe she wasn't the only one speaking in euphemisms.

CHAPTER FOURTEEN

Something practical made no sense, until Chase entered the room carrying clothes. What he should have said was something unappealing. He handed her a pair of sweats. Thick, bulky, and a size too big.

"They belong to my sister. Eve calls them comfort clothes. These and a good book are easier on her diet than Ben and Jerry's."

Since she knew firsthand that Eve was definitely not a large size, C.J. guessed even the rich and famous occasionally had bad days. "Thank you."

In less time than she'd anticipated, she'd stripped out of the silky nightwear and slipped on the softest, thickest sweats she'd ever come in contact with. Slowly turning the knob on the bathroom door, she eased it open and was surprised to see Chase lying on the edge of the bed, shoes off, ankles crossed, and still fully dressed.

"I thought this would be safer."

That made her laugh. He did realize that clothes could easily be removed?

"Come sit." Rather than tap the mattress with his hand, he pointed to the other side of the bed with his chin.

All the apprehension she'd felt since discovering the Baron matriarch had moved her suitcase into Chase's designated room abandoned her. Maybe wearing comfortable—though obviously expensive—sweats, for the first time in days. Or maybe she shared his false sense of security in the protective properties of baggy clothes.

Propping the pillows behind her, she eased onto the opposite edge of the mattress and leaned back. "What did you want to talk about?"

"You."

"Not much to tell."

"Not buying it. I want to know all about you, Cassandra Jane. Why did you tell me you're between jobs?"

She shrugged. She wasn't hiding anything; it was just simpler than explaining. "Because I am."

He didn't speak, just looked at her, waiting.

Grabbing hold of one of the decorative pillows piled between them, she fidgeted with the fringe. In the unwritten rules of life, not talking about what happened in country had to be at the top. A good reason why so many of the people she worked with struggled once they came home. And who was she kidding, thinking she wasn't one of *them*? She'd been home long enough to decompress. By now she should have gotten a nice job in a nice hospital and been helping nice patients get better. Instead she'd taken full advantage of a healthy savings account, and, under the guise of looking out for her somewhat ditzy sister, dug in at Bev's tiny apartment and created her own little deluded sanctuary.

Chase hadn't been the first person to ask her about her work or her time overseas, yet, oddly enough, for the first time since she'd come home, something deep inside her actually wanted to talk. And not just to anyone but to Chase. "I joined up straight out of high school. There aren't many great career opportunities for high school graduates without a college degree, and I couldn't afford the time or the tuition to get one."

Chase nodded but said nothing.

How could he do otherwise? He had no idea at all what it felt like to live hand to mouth, to watch his mother work two jobs just to give her children the bare necessities of life—like food and shelter—never mind pay for higher education.

"Growing up I'd always thought it would be nice to be a doctor. Take care of the sick, cure cancer." She chuckled at her own childhood dreams.

"Don't laugh. I can see you as a doctor."

She shrugged. "I signed up for the Marine Corpsman Field Medical School—"

"You're a Marine?" His eyes rounded wide enough to see perfect circles of white form around that sea of steel blue.

"Technically I'm US Navy, but, for all intents and purposes, I act like, work with, and am treated like a Marine. I had to do seven weeks at Camp Lejeune. Trust me. I know what it's like to be a Marine. The Marines have a saying—every Marine is a rifleman. We had to learn to carry a rifle and how to use it as well. To be an effective medic, I had to earn the right to be regarded as a fellow Marine."

A hint of a smile lifted one corner of his mouth. "And you did, didn't you?"

She nodded. All her fellow corpsmen had. The women had to work harder, faster, and prove themselves better, every damn day. That part never stopped.

"Which also explains why you withstood the Governor in your face so easily."

"I've been dressed down by worse."

The smile slipped from his face. "Tell me more."

"My first tour was one year on a medevac crew in Afghanistan." From the corner of her eye she caught Chase's wince. She tried to stop her mind from going back in time to some of the worst days. Being first responders too often meant dealing with military and civilians alike. Adults and children. "Eventually I became the lead medic for the female engagement team."

"Even without knowing you very long, that doesn't surprise me. And I understand a little better how you just stepped in for your sister. Compared to a war zone, this must be a cake walk."

There was no understanding a war zone for people who hadn't been there. No words. At least none that anyone wanted to share, which is why so many veterans came home with wounds the average eye couldn't see. "At least interacting with your family doesn't require combat training."

"When dealing with the Governor, there are people who would disagree with you. But I don't understand how you could be a medic. I thought women weren't allowed in combat situations."

C.J. almost laughed. Even before the SECDEF opened all jobs to women, females often did as much as their male counterparts. While true that forward-operating bases were surrounded by wire fencing, female medics could and did go outside the line. It was just the reality of war. She hadn't been seen as a *female* medic. She was a medic, and lives depended on her and her teammates. "Things aren't always as they seem. Medics, regardless of gender, are required to accompany soldiers on patrol."

A muscle in Chase's chin twitched.

Focusing on the pillow in her hands instead of the darkening expression on Chase's face, C.J. kept talking. "That part of the world is a desert. Patrolling in body armor in full kit easily created heat casualties. But sixty percent of all coalition casualties were from IEDs. If we could do anything at all, we'd start fluids, control the bleeding, and stabilize them until the birds got there. After a while it wasn't enough. If I was staying in, I wanted to do more. I wanted to be part of the forward surgical team."

"That's when you became a nurse?"

C.J. laughed. "It sounds so easy when you say it. If I

had a do over, I'd find a way to get my Bachelors of Nursing before going in. Getting into a nursing program while active-duty enlisted doesn't happen often. It's hard, competitive, and takes forever—"

"But you did it?"

She couldn't stop herself from smiling if she had wanted to. "I did. We've handled six hundred trauma cases in a single year."

He hissed in another pained breath. "So what happened?"

Everything. Nothing. "The pressure of constant deployments, the stress of saving soldiers' lives—it starts to take its toll. It never stops. If one country isn't the aggressor, then another one takes its turn. One day I realized, if I had to send home, in parts or a body bag, one more boy—because most of these soldiers are just kids—I'd wind up in a padded cell."

Somehow, without her noticing, his hand had breached the distance between them, and Chase had partly covered hers, his thumb making slow rhythmic movements. His gentle concern was soothing in a way nothing else had been.

"When do you go back?" he asked.

"I don't." She chose to ignore his strong hand folded around hers and to draw much-needed strength from him. "I resigned my commission. I had to."

His thumb continued to gently caress the back of her hand. "Then what's the plan?"

"I don't have one."

"Isn't there a nursing shortage in this country?"

C.J. nodded.

"Surely a local hospital has need of a nurse with your skills and background?"

"I don't doubt they do. I just don't know that I can keep doing this. I can't see myself taking temperatures and blood pressure in a doctor's office, and I don't think I have it in me anymore to work in a trauma center or emergency room."

"So, instead, you're pretending to be an idiot's date for a wedding."

"You're not an idiot."

"Don't get me wrong. There's nothing easy about running a Fortune 500 company and answering to an aging, stubborn old man. But none of what I do at my job comes close to the hard work or sacrifices you've had to make."

"Not me." The boys she couldn't save, those were the heroes. "The innocent women and children caught in the crosshairs, no one is telling them *job well done*. Thanking them for their—"

"I'm sorry." He inched up and, settling as close as he could without touching, let his fingers lace with hers. "*Thank you* isn't enough to the men and women who serve. And sacrifice. But you are one heck of a woman, Cassandra J. Lawson."

Pins and needles pricked at Chase's fingers all the way up to his elbow. The faint scent of vanilla tickled his senses. He recognized that scent. It belonged to C.J. As did the weight resting on his forearm.

For hours he'd listened as she had told him story after story of the horrors and successes of being in a war zone and wished he could do something to wipe away the hurt and pain that played in her eyes. Though he distinctly remembered her drifting off with her head on the pillow, sometime in the night C.J. had inched her way closer, until they slept spooned like an old married couple.

And wasn't that an interesting thought. More so, why didn't that thought scare the living heck out of him?

Probably because, when he'd told C.J. that she was one heck of a woman, he wasn't trying to snow her. He'd meant every word. From her kind heart, to her quick mind, to her sense of play, to her loyalty to both family and country, to her ability to stand strong under the heavy weight of the Baron dynasty's leader. Chase's new challenge was, what to do with C. J. Lawson? How could he find a place for her in his world? If she belonged at all.

CHAPTER FIFTEEN

At first light C.J. had been a little surprised to wake and find the bed empty. For a split second she considered she had just dreamed about talking with Chase for hours. She hadn't meant to go into so much detail about herself, but talking to him had been so easy.

Somewhere the conversation had shifted to a history of the Baron family. The great-grandfather's little hotel business that the Governor and his brother had turned into a world wide enterprise and massive family fortune. What it was like for Chase growing up as the eldest in his branch of the Baron clan. The constant need to prove himself to be better than his playboy father. Always setting the example for his younger siblings. The pride and joy in Chase's eyes as he spoke of each of his siblings' successes. The craziness that ensued from Knockout Kyle's affinity for speed, career choice, and playboy tendencies. From the sound of Kyle's escapades, and close calls on the racetrack, C.J. was surprised the entire family didn't have gray hair.

Breakfast at the ranch was almost as elaborate an event as dinner the night before. "Sorry I wasn't there when you woke up." Chase sidled up beside her. "Grandfather wanted to meet with my brothers and me to go over the week's schedule."

"And Eve?"

Chase shook his head. "The Governor is very old-fashioned in more ways than we sometimes like to admit."

"In other words, he's a bit of a chauvinist."

"I wouldn't go that far, but he does believe in taking care of the women in his family."

C.J. shrugged. She'd be lying if she said she hadn't run into more than one Marine who thought women had no place in the military outside of a veteran's hospital, but right now she was in too good a mood to discuss the Governor and any archaic mind-sets. She scooped a steaming spoonful of scrambled eggs from the silver platters on the massive buffet onto a china plate. "Have you eaten yet?"

"With the Governor, yes."

"Oh." Scanning the room, her gaze settled on the massive table and the family members scattered about. From what she'd gathered last night, she, Emily, and Siobhan's young friend were the only non-relatives in attendance. It was one heck of a clan.

"From here we're all heading back to the resort." Chase poured himself a cup of coffee. "The official wedding celebrations begin with grandmother's afternoon tea."

"Good morning." Siobhan came up behind Chase and picked up a plate. "I really am sorry for intruding last night. I thought you had your own room."

"No problem, kiddo." Chase flicked the tip of her nose. "We were just talking."

Siobhan batted at his hand. "Right. Just talking."

"Talking," Chase enunciated clearly.

Shaking her head, Siobhan rolled her eyes. "Mum would tan my hide if she caught me up close and personal and I gave her an excuse like *just talking*."

Chase opened his mouth and immediately snapped it shut. He was a smart man, smart enough to realize he could not win this debate with his kid sister.

"Devlin thinks we can take the *Fidelis* out Thursday when the rest of the family is on the *Baroness*."

"And who's going to talk the Governor into that one?"

His hand on C.J.'s lower back, Chase guided her to the table, Siobhan on his heels.

"Why, me of course!" The girl's grin took over her face. C.J. could see why Chase had a soft spot for his youngest half sibling. She had a warmth about her that spread out and hugged the people around her.

"You probably are the only one who could."

Siobhan took the seat beside C.J. "Has Chase told you about the *Fidelis*?"

C.J. shook her head. They'd had other things on their minds last night.

"It's a fifty-foot racing yacht. Devlin and Chase were runners-up with her in the America's Cup."

C.J. turned to Chase. He'd made no mention of sailing. Or racing.

Chase shrugged. "It was a very long time ago."

Where Chase was modest, his youngest sister was full of information. C.J. learned all about the vessel, how it was Chase who taught Kyle the art of racing, and how after the sailboat had been retired from the racing circuit, the interior had been refitted for more comfort, but she could still fly on a windy day. It quickly became clear to C.J. that Siobhan adored Chase. The young woman practically glowed with pride for her brother's accomplishments and could barely sit still at the prospect of him and his cousin Devlin letting her help crew the sailboat. The young man with Siobhan, Michael, a cousin on her mother's side, ate like a true frat boy with a hollow leg, only glancing up to offer the occasional smile before diving back into the mound of food on his plate.

C.J. was on her last bite of French toast when Eve came up behind them.

"Craig and I are heading out in a few. The Governor and Grams are all set also."

Chase looked C.J.'s way and, only with his eyes, asked

if she was ready. With a quick nod, she set her napkin on the table beside her and pushed her seat back.

"Come on, Michael." Siobhan stood, tugging at her cousin's sleeve. "We'll follow them."

"We who?" Chase frowned.

"That would be me, sir," Michael spoke his first words since inhaling his food.

"On the wrong side of the road?" Chase's words straddled a fine line between teasing and reprimand.

"Opposite, sir. But I do fine on the right side. Siobhan's mum made sure of that before she let me drive us here from DFW."

"Except for the windshield wipers." Siobhan laughed. And Michael shot her a stern glance. "Sorry," she added with a bit of unrepentant mischief in her eyes.

"Habit had me reaching for the wipers instead of the turn signal a time or two. But I can assure you, it has not been a problem. I've corrected in sufficient time for other drivers to know my intentions."

"And we have a very clean windshield." Siobhan's eyes flashed with humor. This time C.J. smiled with her, though Chase hadn't been drawn in.

"You should ride with us," Chase finally said.

Siobhan's gaze went from amused to determined in a heartbeat. "Now don't you go all paternal on me. We're not competing in a grand prix. Besides, each car is full."

"That's right," Eve interjected. "The Governor and Grams want to ride with you and C.J."

Chase's head whipped around. "What?"

"You heard me. He sent the limo ahead with Oliver's family. And, for what it's worth, we rode behind Siobhan on the way here. Michael did just fine."

The young man smiled appreciatively at Eve but said nothing.

The Governor's cane thumped on the hardwood floors

as he entered the dining room. "Let's get this show on the road."

Yes, indeed, and what a show it was going to be.

"Did you know Michael is driving Siobhan?" Chase addressed his grandfather in the passenger seat of the car.

"I did. He's accompanied Siobhan to the States before. He's proven to be a sound driver and solid travel companion."

Despite the Governor's reassurance, being reminded that his little sister wasn't little any more left Chase feeling anything but assured. "Maybe, but I still don't have to like it."

The Governor's stoic expression didn't change, but Chase could see his grandmother smiling in the backseat.

"You'll make an excellent father," Grams said, delight dancing in her eyes.

"Grandmother," Chase admonished softly. He wished he could see all of C.J.'s face. He didn't know which would be worse, having his grandfather grill his date or his grandmother kill her with not-so-subtle innuendoes.

"Did you enjoy your stay, dear?"

C.J. bobbed her head. "Very much, thank you."

"The house is quite adequate for our little family. Though there are plans ready to expand as the family continues to grow. You know, room for great-grandchildren."

C.J. nodded. Chase sighed.

"We are so looking forward to having small children in the house again." His grandmother directed her comment to Chase and then turned a softer smile on C.J.

"Listen to your grandmother," the Governor bellowed

beside him. "You've all played around long enough. It's time to get serious. You've got a nice girl here—"

"Governor!" Chase should have insisted Eve and Mitch take the Governor and their grandmother.

"Don't you Governor me. You're five years older than Andrew. It's time, boy. It's time. Do you like children?" The Governor asked over his shoulder.

"Doesn't everyone?"

"Starting to wonder," the Governor mumbled. "I should have a passel of little children around on holidays and weekends."

"Governor," Chase cut in, "with Andrew and Nancy marrying you'll have great grands soon enough."

And so went the conversation for the next hour, battling back and forth, with Chase making every effort to redirect conversation to anyone besides himself and C.J. And, bless her, she held up like a trooper. Fit in well. Very well. So well that, by the time they pulled into the parking lot at the resort, C.J. had the Governor retelling in painful detail the path of Baron Enterprises into the prosperous business Chase ran today. But rather than Chase finding her eyes glazed over with boredom, the Governor held her attention. She'd asked key questions at the right moments and had the Governor smiling more in the short car ride than Chase had seen at countless family dinners. Apparently he wasn't the only Baron man who C.J. was winning over.

Chase blew out another relieved breath as Michael pulled up to the resort entrance. Siobhan climbed out of the car, leaned into the passenger window for just a second, and then turned to continue inside while her cousin headed to a shady spot in the lot to park.

With both his aging grandparents in the car, Chase pulled into the handicapped spot. Engine running, he hopped out to open his grandmother's door, and C.J. went for the Governor's. Chase didn't know if the Governor recognized her stance or not, but now Chase realized she tended to stand at what he believed to be parade rest. Straight, steady, and ready to spring into action. A watchful eye on the old man, insistent on exiting the car unassisted, C.J. was prepared to step in if needed.

Focusing on his grandmother's slower steps as they circled the car, Chase almost didn't hear the unusually loud rumble of an engine. Not until he heard C.J.'s voice scream, "incoming," did he look up to see C.J. curled around his grandfather, her back to a full-size black sedan speeding down from between the rows of parked cars and flying past them.

The crackle of shattering glass echoed around them, immediately followed by crunching and crashing noises and one blood-curdling scream.

CHAPTER SIXTEEN

C.J. had taken off running at a full gallop, Chase only inches behind her.

The once beautiful lobby was covered in dust, broken glass, cracked woodwork, two-by-fours, and broken sheetrock. The place looked like a junkyard. Except for the shaken people, huddled together for protection from the unknown assault. Tears, prayers, and cries of pain transported C.J. across the world to a time and place where destruction and death were an everyday part of her life.

Physically shaking away the images, she did a fast scan, seeking out the area of impact and the most likely place to find the worst casualties, her heart rate easing with every person who stood unharmed and shook off the dust. A tall man C.J. didn't recognize leaned into the open door of the mangled vehicle shaking his head. The driver was dead. Moving quickly C.J. continued seeking out the injured.

"What the heck?" One of the Baron brothers came running in the open space that used to be a wall.

"Head wound," she called out over a young man, sitting, knees up, staring blankly at the room, a tiny stream of blood slowly making its way down his cheek. "Medic!" she yelled unthinking, quickly bending down for a better look before realizing there would be no medic to help.

Chase knelt down beside her. "What do you need?"

After a quick assessment of the bleeding wound, she looked at Chase. "Superficial. Pressure will be fine till help arrives."

Mitch Baron came running over. "I'll take care of this."

C.J. pushed to her feet, working her way at a brisk trot to the registration desk, where the car had come to a forced stop, thankful for minimum casualties. Bruises and broken bones she could deal with. And then she saw it. The growing red blotch on a dusty gray canvas. Running, she skidded to a stop at the limp body near the runaway vehicle.

Siobhan.

The pool of blood on her thigh grew. Fast. Too fast. The femoral artery. *Damn.* Whipping off her blouse C.J. placed the top over the life-threatening gash and leaned with all her weight on the injured leg, turning to whoever stood to her side in men's dress shoes. "Give me your tie. Now." With both hands pressed hard against the still-gushing wound, she looked to the tan trousers on her other side. "Get down here. Press here as hard as you can. I need to get a tourniquet on this leg fast."

Chase knelt down beside her. "Like this?"

His hands covered hers, and she wished for a split second that she could use the electricity that always sparked between them to cauterize the wound. What a raw deal. "Yes. Like that."

A brown tie now dangled in front of her. As fast as her fingers could work, she wrapped it around Siobhan's thigh, twisted it tightly against the wound, inserted a nearby splintered piece of wood, then twisted it even tighter before tying a knot. She had to stop the circulation completely. C.J. prayed losing the leg wouldn't be the price of saving Siobhan's life.

To no one in particular C.J. called out, "I need something to raise her feet. Pillows, cushions, anything. She's going into shock." Siobhan was still losing blood at an alarming rate, and it was vital to get what blood she did have left going to the brain and major organs instead of to her extremities. "What's the ETA on an ambulance?"

Kyle held up his phone. "Not happening. A tractor-trailer overturned on the bridge taking several cars with it. Lots of casualties. All emergency vehicles available are on that accident scene. Access to Houston is blocked. No one can get in or out. I've got the helicopter on *The Baroness* coming this way."

A couple of large pillows in expensive Egyptian cotton were shoved at her. She recognized the intense Baron gaze. Another brother. "Thanks."

Still on her knees she placed both pillows under the youngest Baron sister's feet. The kid was going deeper into shock. She'd lost too much blood already. *Damn it.*

She needed the bird here *now* before time ran out on the leg. Scanning quickly for more injuries on the teen, her attention landed on Siobhan's face. Her lips were turning blue. *Crud.* C.J. pinched off the girl's nose and tilted back her head before giving her two quick breaths, sealing Siobhan's lips with her own.

The expected rush of air didn't come—no chest movement. *Blast. She's obstructed.* Facing the surrounding crowd, C.J. needed help. Fast. "I need a knife. Some kind of narrow tube—a pen, a hard straw."

People around her dispersed in the quiet chaos. All she heard was a muffled chorus of "I'm on that," tumbling over "In my bag" and "Be right back." The *be right back* better be fast as heck, or she would lose this sweet young woman.

Rubble shifted beside her as a disposable cup with a straw was thrust in her face. "Does it matter if I drank from it?"

"No." She snatched the straw. "I'll need tape too. And alcohol. Any kind, I don't care. Booze will do."

More items began appearing before her. A hunting knife. Packing tape. No alcohol. "Anyone got a match or lighter?" What had been no more than a few seconds felt like an eternity. Siobhan's lips had turned a darker shade of blue. *Stay with me, Siobhan.* C.J. hadn't come thousands of miles to still send kids home in a body bag *or* in parts.

A red Bic dangled in front of her, and she heard a scolding female voice huff, "Arthur, you promised to quit," followed by the immediate response of "Aren't you glad I didn't?" The pissed-off woman had no comeback, but, right about now, C.J. was very happy about it, because, so far, the knife tip would be the only thing even slightly close to sterile.

Heavy footsteps stomped from behind. "Here's some Jack Daniel's."

"Thanks." She had no idea who she was thanking. Grabbing the bottle, she dumped half of it over the knife blade and her patient's neck, then located the cricoid cartilage, and made a horizontal incision in Siobhan's neck. Quickly she sliced the straw in half and inserted it into the incision. At the swoosh of air, instant hope pulsed through C.J.'s veins. She wasn't a surgeon, and this wasn't a sterile OR, but at least bombs weren't blowing up around them. She'd worked in worse conditions than this to stabilize the patient. *The golden hour.* God, how she hated that. The small window to save lives until they could be sent somewhere and patched up right.

Confident the trach tube worked well enough for now, C.J. checked the injured leg again. The bleeding had stopped. So had the circulation. They were running out of time to save the leg. Where the heck was that helo?

The longer Chase waited in the emergency room with his immediate family, the more fear and panic slowly gave way to hope. He and C.J. had arrived with Siobhan. C.J. hadn't said anything during the flight, but he knew from the look in her eyes that she was worried. The helicopter made additional trips to bring his siblings and grandparents. The cousins waited at the resort. Once the bridge was cleared, he knew the remainder of the Baron clan would come. The Governor may have played hardball most of their lives, but he made sure every Baron understood that family was the secret weapon in the war on life.

The double doors opened, and C.J. walked out of the emergency area, dressed in scrubs.

"They gave me something clean to wear," she explained.

Chase nodded. "You were amazing."

Blinking a few times, she surprised him by stepping up and dropping her forehead on his shoulder.

Circling her in his arms, Chase ran his fingers through her hair. He didn't know what to say. Or if he should even speak at all. But holding her felt right. To anyone else it might look like he was the one offering her strength and comfort, when, in truth, having her in his arms gave him the strength he needed. Not until this very second did he realize how badly he'd shortchanged himself in life. Was it possible to fall in love with someone in only a few days? To know so little about them and yet feel as though he knew everything he needed to know?

C.J. shifted in place, turning her cheek to rest against his heartbeat, winding her arms around him.

Oh, yeah. This was definitely the big *L*. There were very few things he was sure of in life. Death, which he hoped to God they wouldn't experience today. Taxes. And standing here, breathing as one with C.J., he was sure he could never go back to the way his life was before. C. J. Lawson was meant to be his. Now all he had to do was convince her of that.

CHAPTER SEVENTEEN

C.J. had no idea how much time had passed since Siobhan had been wheeled to the OR and when C.J. had then settled in the safety of Chase's embrace. He'd held her quietly until finally suggesting they sit down. Still hanging on to him with one arm, they moved as one to the waiting room chairs, and, once seated, she'd laid her head on his shoulder, and he kept an arm draped possessively around her. No one spoke. The proverbial pin could have been heard falling to the tile floor.

At least Siobhan had been alive when they'd arrived—barely, but alive. That was something. And now C.J. clung to the old adage: *no news is good news*. If the doctors lost Siobhan in surgery, someone would have come out to speak to them by now. If Siobhan was still hanging on, then she was strong enough to get through this. Of that C.J. was sure. The question tearing at her again and again was, had she done enough? Would Siobhan keep her leg?

And then C.J. felt it. The tender touch of Chase's lips to the top of her head. Not a sensual touch but rather a gesture of comfort. Almost as if he knew she was heading down the slippery road of self-doubt and needed uplifting. The simple kiss made her feel totally and completely cared for. Cherished. Loved. And she liked it. A whole lot. More than she should, because, like it or not, negotiated or not, C.J. was falling in love with Chase Baron.

"Governor Baron?" a man asked, and C.J. lifted her

gaze and noticed the others were already standing, waiting to hear what the doctor had to say. "Your granddaughter is doing better than we could expect. I see no reason she shouldn't have a full recovery."

Instantly the thick tension hanging in the steady silence evaporated. Hugs, smiles, and manly backslapping were happily exchanged.

In order to let Chase stand with his family, C.J. lifted her head and pulled away, only he didn't move. Didn't stand to hear what else the doctor might say. He sat, staring at her, studying her. The strength of his gaze made her warm all over. How the heck was she supposed to walk away in a few days and pretend she'd never had Chase Baron in her life?

"Which one of you administered first aid?" Tall, older, and with graying hair, the doctor's booming voice matched his rugged appearance.

Chase nodded at her and smiled. Slowly she pushed to her feet and walked to the huddle of family members. Chase remained at her side, his reassuring hand resting at the small of her back. He was here for her. "She did."

The doctor studied her for a moment before responding, "Excellent work under the circumstances. You saved her life *and* the leg."

For the first time in hours, a smile pulled at her cheeks. "Good."

"What's your background?"

"Lt. C. J. Lawson, US Navy. Three tours in country."

The doctor pressed his lips together and dipped his chin in a single motion. "When Uncle Sam has had enough of you, come see me."

C.J. nodded politely. The strangling lack of breath that usually assailed her whenever she talked of finding a civilian nursing job didn't come. Maybe she was ready to move on. Or maybe she was still numb from the recent adrenaline surge.

"Does anyone know what the heck happened?" Mitch asked.

Kyle nodded. "Looks like the driver, a registered guest, had a heart attack while behind the wheel. No other serious injuries. Crews are already on-site, cleaning up."

Eve leaned against her brother Craig. "I keep thinking how much worse this could have been if Siobhan had been standing just a few inches to the left. That car could have mowed her down."

Mitch pulled away from the crowd and walked over to C.J. "Thank you. If you hadn't been there, I don't think any of us would have realized how serious her injury was."

"And none of us would have been able to do what you did." Eve eased around her brother and pulled C.J. into a hug. "Thank you."

One by one, C.J. found herself nearly crushed in a wealth of Baron appreciation.

"Lieutenant." The Governor tapped his cane on the floor.

"Sir." Habit had C.J. snapping her heels and standing at attention.

"At ease, woman." Like the Red Sea, the family parted, making room for the Governor. "I knew I liked you. No matter what this foolish grandson of mine does, you're part of this family. Remember that."

C.J. nodded. If only Chase felt the same way.

Not until Siobhan had opened her eyes, and C.J. could see for herself that her patient really would be okay, did CJ agree to be taken home to the suite. Showered and changed into their own clean clothes, they'd spent the rest of the evening curled up on the sofa, watching a marathon of romantic comedies. As each movie ended, he could feel a little more of the tension in C.J.'s body seeping away.

By the time room service brought dinner, the dark shadows that had haunted her eyes all day were replaced with a glimmer of light. As the night swallowed the last ray of daylight, the need for quiet had passed, and they'd shared more stories. Chase told her about the year he and Devlin raced in the America's Cup. She shared stories about what it was like being the average-smart sister to a beauty queen.

The Governor had arranged for Siobhan's mother Maura to be flown in on a company jet. They'd finished My Cousin Vinny and were about to begin The Last Holiday with Queen Latifah when a light rap sounded at the door.

"I'll get it." As much as Chase regretted easing away from the comfortable hold he had on CJ, she still looked exhausted and didn't want her getting the door.

To his surprise, Maura stood at the other side. "I hope it's not too late."

"No of course not." Chase waved her in. "Is everything okay with Siobhan?" He was positive if she'd taken a turn for the worse, someone would have reached out to him, but he didn't understand why Maura was here.

"She's fine. Sleeping like a baby. The doctors practically threw me out."

That didn't sound right. "I'll make a call."

"No." She extended her arm. "It's okay. I'm going to shower, change out of these clothes, maybe grab a snack and head back. I know she's going to be sleeping all night, but I still want to be by my baby's side."

"Of course. I'll make sure there's a driver on hand."

Again, the woman held her hand out to him and shook her head. "The Governor has taken care of everything I just wanted to take a minute to thank CJ."

From the first exchange of conversation, CJ had pushed

to her feet and eased her way to the suites foyer. "I'm glad I was there."

"So am I." Her last word came out in a sob as Maura almost collapsed into CJ's arms. "I can't imagine life without my baby."

"It's okay." CJ held on to Siobhan's mother and Chase was in the awkward position of being at a loss for what to do or say.

Being at the head of the family business for nearly a decade, making decisions on facts was easy. How to comfort a mother who came within inches of losing her only daughter was outside his skill set and not for the first time today, he was very grateful to have CJ at his side.

Maura pulled back, swiped at her eyes and then searching in her pockets, shook her head and muttered, "Oh feck. I know I had a tissue here somewhere."

"Here." Chase pulled a hanky from his pocket. A throw back to the days of chivalry, every once in a blue moon he was glad he always carried one. Today was no exception.

Wiping the tears from her face, Maura smiled at him. "You were always her favorite."

All he could do was smile. All his siblings held a piece of his heart, but Siobhan's piece might be a smidgeon bigger than some of the others.

"I'd better get going."

CJ shook her head. "You're welcome to stay as long as you like. As a matter of fact we were just getting ready to make some popcorn and watch a lighthearted movie. Care to join us?"

Gently running her hand along CJ's cheek, Maura smiled and sighed. "Thank you for the offer, but I want to get back to the hospital. The doctor told me that without you, we would have lost Siobhan. I needed to say thank you in person."

Squeezing her eyes shut for a moment, CJ nodded. "I'm

glad I was here."

"Me too." Maura took a step back. "I'll let you two enjoy your movie."

"We'll be at the hospital in the morning."

"Eve is with her now. I think there's going to be a revolving door of family until she's discharged."

"I'm sure." Chase resisted the urge to pull CJ into his side and instead escorted his one time stepmother to the door. "If you need anything at all. No matter what time. Just let me know."

A few more polite exchanges and Chase closed the door behind his father's ex wife.

"You okay?" Her hand on his shoulder, CJ leaned up against him.

"I am now." He pulled her hand into the fold of his and thanked the heavens for bringing this woman into his life. Returning to the sofa and large screen TV, a bowl of parmesan popcorn in his lap, and CJ tucked warmly against him, they let the heaviness of the day roll away. They'd laughed and smiled and talked some more until the stress of the day seemed to be oh so long ago. Definitely, he was going to need to make some changes in his life and somehow he had to convince CJ to be a part of them.

CHAPTER EIGHTEEN

Tuesday morning came bright and early. The two of them had fallen asleep on the couch and woken at the first ray of sunshine peppering the large room. Despite the chaos of the day before, today had gone mostly as scheduled. Any family not involved in some part of the pre-wedding plans took turns sitting with Siobhan and her mother. CJ understood it was the Baron family in full support mode.

"Yes, sir. I see. Excellent. Yes, sir." Chase nodded.

Eve leaned into CJ. "Clearly it's the Governor on the line."

"How can you tell?" Nancy sitting at the same table for lunch where they'd all met that first night, looked at Eve with furrowed brows.

"Too many sirs in one conversation to be anyone else." Eve shrugged.

"Well." Chase slid his phone into his pocket. "Youth has its advantage. Siobhan is making fabulous progress."

"Wow. That's wonderful." Eve grinned.

"The good news is that she will be discharged in a few days."

Nancy slapped her hands together. "Oh, that's fantastic."

"Yes." Chase took his seat at CJ's side. "And if she stays on the same recovery path, they'll let her attend the wedding too."

"Oh," Eve did a fist bump. "That is good news."

"The downside of course is that she won't be in any shape to be one of the bridesmaids."

Nancy nodded. "We figured as much."

"Will it be a problem to be down one bridesmaid?" Eve asked. "I've seen uneven numbers of bridal parties. Where one person escorts two."

"I thought about that. That could work, but what I really would like," Nancy swiveled in place to face CJ. "I know it's asking a lot, but it seems somehow fitting that you take Siobhan's place in the bridal party."

"Me?" C.J. had almost fallen out of her chair with surprise.

"That is a fantastic idea." Eve rubbed her hands together enthusiastically. "And I know that we can have the dress altered to fit you."

"That's true. You and Siobhan are the same height. The seamstress will have to make a few tucks here and there, but I know she can do it."

"I don't know." CJ shook her head. Words weren't coming fast enough. There were a lot of things in life she was prepared for, walking down the aisle, the lone squid in a sea of fashion model women was not one of them.

"Of course you can," Nancy ran on with all the reasons that it was a brilliant and perfect idea and absolutely appropriate under the circumstances of CJ having saved Siobhan's life.

CJ wasn't sure which she was more uncomfortable with, everyone giving her credit for saving Siobhan, or having to wear an evening gown *and* be the focal point of a few hundred wedding guests until the bride appeared on the aisle. As both Eve and Nancy continued to barrage her with all their good reasons, she glanced in Chase's direction. The man sat at his brother Mitch's side, arms crossed, smiling. When his gaze leveled with hers, he merely shrugged. She got the distinct impression that he was politely telling her she might as well accept that the Baron women were a force of nature. With both Nancy and Eve on the bridesmaid-stand-in bandwagon, C.J. hadn't stood a chance.

As a matter of fact, she hadn't stood a chance with pretty much anything that came to pass. Whenever possible, Chase's grandparents had paired C.J. with Chase over each day's events. Despite her horror when initially told about the doubles tennis match, it turned out C.J. wielded a pretty mean backhand.

"See." Chase gave her a thumbs up from his place across the court. "Told you there was nothing to worry about."

Even though she'd missed a few shots here and there, she was eternally grateful she hadn't tripped over her own two feet and face planted on the court. She was however a little more than excited at how often she managed to not only hit the ball over the net, but hit it so hard and clean that neither Devlin nor his sister Leah could return the volley. She had no idea when or how, but she wouldn't mind working a tennis game or two into her regular workout routine. Though who was she kidding? Once the wedding was over, tennis would have no place in her world. In the end, Devlin and his sister won the Baron Cup.

"I really thought the cup would be ours." Chase wiped his brow with a towel. "You sure you never played before?"

She shook her head. "Never. I guess it's that hand to eye coordination that makes me a good marksmen."

"Could be." He leaned in and kissed her on the nose. "Or you're a natural."

That she wasn't so sure of. What she was sure of, was that she didn't want this day to end. And wasn't that just a darn shame.

Even though CJ insisted she had no natural athletic ability, as it turned out the next day, she fared well on the water too. Even though the navy didn't use sailing ships, C.J. was steady on her feet and eager to jump in and help. Strong winds had given the *Fidelis*, the Governor's favorite seventy-five-foot racing yacht, the power of the gods. At one point, in a friendly little show of strength, the *Fidelis* and a neighbor's boat had raced in spurts. When the sailboat tipped to nearly 85 degrees as the wind filled the sails and carried her across the waves, C.J.'s laughter roared through the rushing wind and wrapped itself tightly around Chase's heart. He vowed at that moment, if she'd let him, he would keep her happy like this for the rest of her life.

"Oh, my God, that was so much fun." C.J. nearly bounced in place. "No wonder Siobhan loves to sail. What a rush."

"Not the same as those big Navy ships?" he teased.

"Not even close." Soaked from head to toe, she used a colorful towel to dry off. "Do you think anyone will take the boat out again before the wedding?"

What she wasn't saying, was before their time together ended. He could see the shadow in her eyes when that same thought crossed her mind as well.

"I'm sure we can fit in another run. Maybe we can even bring Siobhan onboard. As a passenger. No crewing allowed."

"She'd like that." Her smile reached her eyes and he knew that she cared more about Siobhan than herself. He'd learned a lot about this lady in the last few days. With every passing hour he grew more sure of his feelings for C.J. For the first time in his life, he truly believed his grandfather had indeed fallen in love with his future wife at the very moment he'd laid eyes on her, just the way he always said. Though Chase hadn't understood it before now, just like a bird flying south for winter, an instinct deep in his gut had drawn him to C.J.'s side that first night. And now, less than a week later, he couldn't imagine not having her with him. Only two more nights and, unless he came up with a plan, his time with C.J. would be over. Whatever he did, he'd better do it fast, or life after Saturday would not be pretty.

C.J. tossed her beach bag on the sofa and strolled toward the kitchen. "Want anything to drink?"

"Water would be great." Chase's footsteps sounded behind her at the same time her cell phone rang.

"Would you grab that? It might be Bev." Just inside the kitchen doorway, she exchanged his bottled water for her cell. "Hello?"

"C.J.?"

The voice sounded familiar. "Yes?"

"Do you have any idea how hard you've been to track down? Finally convinced your mom to give me your number."

"Captain Miller?"

"You're not in the navy anymore, C.J. Call me Debra."

C.J. dared a look at Chase. Standing only a couple of feet in front of her, his relaxed stance had shifted to one of tense concern. "Nice to hear from you, … Debra."

"Good, because I'm calling on business. Grapevine has it that you're decompressing with your sister."

C.J. nodded before she realized the captain couldn't see her. "Something like that."

"Well, I need a head surgical nurse. A good one."

Her gaze dropped down to the floor, and she spun

around to retrieve her water. "Excuse me?"

"You heard me. I'm offering you a job. Here at Bethesda." Her cheery voice dropped to a lower, more serious octave. "C.J., these men and women still need us. You're too good not to be working."

"I …" Holding the bottle of water in one hand, she turned to face Chase again. He hadn't moved any closer, but he still listened carefully. "I don't know."

"I've got to fill the spot. Will you at least think about it?"

Would she? Did she want to return to the OR? Work with sick and injured veterans? It had been days since Siobhan's accident, and that strangling lack of breath that had previously affected C.J. at the thought of returning to work was nowhere to be found. Adrenaline over Siobhan's injuries had also long since died down. Could it be she really was ready to go back to work? "Yes. Yes, I'll think about it."

"Good." Debra Miller's uplifting tone returned. "I can only hold it open for another few days before I have to make a decision, but I'm hoping you'll say yes."

"Thank you, Cap—Debra."

C.J. flipped her phone case shut and stood frozen, staring down at it, until Chase's fingertips barely grazed the side of her arms. "Everything okay?"

Raising her eyes to meet his, she took a minute to gather thoughts that wouldn't come and shrugged.

"Was it bad news?" His eyes grew cloudy with concern.

"No." She shook her head. "It was a job offer."

Chase's hands fell to his side. "A good one?"

"Could be. In Maryland."

Eyes that had been narrowed in serious thought widened then returned to normal, almost indifferent.

Did he not care? Had they not grown as close as she'd thought over these last few days? What was going through his mind? "I don't know what to do."

With his hand curled inward, he ran the back of his knuckles across her chin. "What do you want to do?"

Meeting his questioning gaze, she waited for her gut to talk to her. "I think I want to say yes."

CHAPTER NINETEEN

The wedding day had finally arrived, and C.J. was horribly torn. She'd enjoyed every one of the scheduled events way more than she had expected to. Every Baron had been very kind to her from the beginning, but, since the accident with Siobhan, C.J. had actually begun to feel like a member of the family.

No one was more surprised than her to discover that those few weeks of summer camp had left her with one heck of a backhand in tennis. And though she knew she had no issues with boats and motion sickness, she hadn't been prepared to love sailing so much. Definitely not a poor man's sport. Chatting with the crew, she was flabbergasted at the cost of racing a yacht and even more taken aback at the cost of the actual sailboat, of which, the Barons owned more than one.

The Baron family wealth was simply mind-boggling. And yet being around them felt so normal. They laughed and cried and worried and played and danced and ate and loved, just like everyone else. And they gave. Despite her initial frustration with the amount of money Chase spent— from a valet service to park his car in an empty lot to the clothes on her back she would probably never wear again— she'd since learned that the Baron family followed the philosophy of those blessed with much are responsible for much.

Besides running Fortune 500 companies or managing

successful careers, every single member of the Baron family was involved in major charity work. Some sat on various boards of directors, and others were more hands-on with favorite causes, but everyone, including the teens, were responsible for giving back. Chase was the head of more than one cause. C.J. had no idea how he divided his time in so many ways, and she probably would never find out.

Over the two days since sailing and her phone call from Debra, C.J. had hoped he'd say or do something that hinted he wanted to extend their deal. Make it more personal. She wanted to return to nursing, but she could do that anywhere. Working for Captain Miller would be a no-brainer. The woman was a phenomenal surgeon and wonderful mentor. But she wasn't the only good boss in the country.

Chase had been sympathetic and supportive, both before and after the call. A few times she'd caught him watching her with that look that turned her insides to jelly. More than once she'd have sworn he might even kiss her— for real. But nothing. No hint or clue came that he had any intention of changing their business agreement. So she'd plastered on a brave face and carried on, determined to enjoy every minute of whatever little time they had left. Including this morning.

"I can't believe we need all day to get ready for the wedding." C.J. pushed away from the small breakfast table.

"All I know is that there are strict orders for all the women to report to the spa by 10:00 a.m. I'm not privy to whatever torture, er, plans you're in store for." Chase flashed a cheesy smile.

She hated that most of her last day in this world of make believe had to be spent away from Chase. "It's not like it'll take all day to do *my* hair." The whole point of her cropped cut was to be able to wash and wear.

"My job is merely to make sure you're on time. Then I join my brothers to make sure Andrew doesn't run away from home."

The serious look on Chase's face made C.J. do a double take. "You don't really …?"

"No." Chase smiled. "Andrew is so into Nancy that I'm often amazed he can breathe when she's not in the room."

"They are pretty smitten."

"It's almost annoying."

"Almost?"

Chase shrugged. "I can't be annoyed about anyone or anything that makes my cousin so happy."

C.J. flashed back to Chase's earlier comment about not being happy deep down. Funny how appearances could be deceiving. To C.J., everyone looked happy this week. Except for the day the runaway car almost killed Siobhan, she mostly felt like she was in the happiest place on earth.

"Ready?" Chase stood at the door.

She slung her purse strap over her shoulder and forced a smile. "You really don't need to come with me. I can find my way."

Chase pinned her with his gaze, but, like every time before, instead of reaching out, he took a retreating step. How had he gone from comforting caresses to keeping his distance? And how could she change that before tomorrow morning's departure?

"Wow." Eve grinned at her future cousin-in-law. "Andrew will swallow his tongue when he sees you."

"Everyone looks wonderful." Nancy peered over her shoulder at the women who had spent the better part of the day being primped and coifed for the evening wedding ceremony. C.J. didn't doubt they all looked fabulous. Anyone who spent an entire day at the resort's spa getting worked over, literally from head to toe, should look like a million bucks.

When the makeup artist finished doing her eyes, C.J. wasn't sure she could open her eyelids. She'd never worn so much makeup in her life and darned if she didn't look almost good enough to compete in one of her sister's beauty pageants. Even her military-length haircut appeared stylish and feminine. And the dress that Nancy had flown in and altered for C.J. made her look like a goddess. But even stranger than her transformation from battle-ready soldier to princess was that—rather than feeling out of place like a badly dressed-up Barbie doll—C.J. felt absolutely beautiful.

The first notes of the wedding music began to play. This was the cue the bridal party had been waiting for. Lowest in the pecking order among the bridesmaids, C.J. was first out the door. The row of Baron men at the foot of the altar was an impressive sight. Each with broad shoulders, varying shades of chestnut hair, and deep soulful eyes, the Baron men had enough testosterone pinging about to make every woman in the church weak in the knees. To keep her own steps steady, C.J. tried to focus on the groom. Andrew Baron Miller was charming, handsome, and the anticipation in his eyes warmed C.J.'s heart. In contrast, every time her gaze drifted to the man beside him, her heart took off in double time.

Taking her place at the opposite side of the altar from the men, she resisted the urge to glance across the way and instead kept her focus on the shift in music and the beautiful bride standing in the vestibule doorway. Nancy was stunning; Andrew was grinning, and blast if C.J. didn't need to take a quick peek at Chase.

He was watching her. Every eye in the church was on Nancy, except Chase's. He hadn't looked away. Every time C.J. glanced in his direction, their eyes met, and her toes curled. Maybe she could look for work in Dallas. Find an excuse to run into Chase. Or maybe she should put away pie-in-the-sky dreams and come back down to reality. Her pretend time was nearly over.

The moon shone brightly over the beach. Nancy's mom had argued to hold the reception at her country club, but Nancy had loved the idea of an intimate beach wedding. A challenge with a guest list of almost five hundred people and another excellent reason that a country club reception would be the most logical locale. Except when marrying a Baron. Anything was possible for a Baron. It was a privilege Chase had been well aware of since he was old enough to make sense of the world around him. And one thing he'd learned from watching his grandfather and grandmother was that nothing was too much for a Baron man to arrange if it made the woman he loved happy.

Andrew had immediately worked everything out, including convincing the Governor that the Baron guest list didn't need to be five-hundred strong. A company from upstate was brought in to set up a tent suitable for Barnum & Bailey on the only section of beachfront property large enough to support the slightly—barely—smaller crowd for the reception. Now sneaking a quiet moment alone under the moonlight, Andrew and Nancy had never looked happier, and they'd looked pretty darn happy before.

"Make up your mind yet?" Craig handed his brother Chase a cold bottle of beer and followed his gaze to the lone couple dancing on the sand.

"Thanks." He accepted the drink. "About what?"

"C.J."

Chase shifted his attention to the shoreline and the torches forming a trail to the beach. With some kind of gauze fabric tied out of the way, the tent offered a breathtaking 360-degree view to the water and surrounding resort. Despite the size of the crowd, the ambiance was somehow intimate, romantic, and exactly the setting that his new cousin-in-law had wanted. Even if she and Andrew had slipped away from it all for a few minutes for a private dance. The resort's wedding planner had done a fabulous job. She'd even easily appeased the Governor's few demands and still gave Nancy her dream wedding.

"Don't tell me you're still thinking about it," Craig continued.

"No. I'm not."

"So what are you going to do?"

"Now? Nothing."

Craig's bottle stopped halfway to his mouth. "You're going to give her up?"

Chase was a Baron. There was no reason he couldn't move heaven and earth for the woman he loved. Whatever it took to make her happy, he'd do it. Even if it meant living in Maryland. He set his own bottle on the table beside him. "I've never given up on anything in my life."

CHAPTER TWENTY

Seated on the opposite side of the dais from Chase, casually exchanging glances had been impossible without obviously leaning forward and staring at him. The last dinner plates had been cleared, and the band announced the dance for the bride and groom. C.J. almost had tears in her eyes when she noticed Andrew singing along with the band. She didn't have to read lips to know he was repeating every word of John Legend's love song "All of Me" to his new wife. When they moved around far enough, C.J. could see Nancy singing back. They might as well have been the only two people in the room.

For the next song, Five for Fighting's "100 Years," the bridal party was called from their seats onto the floor. Andrew and Nancy never took their eyes off each other, and C.J. ached for one dance with Chase. The romantic melody filled the air as she spun into Mitch's hold. Nancy's maid of honor was dancing with Chase. Eve was paired with Craig. Another soulful rhythm kicked in, inviting all the guests to dance, and C.J. found herself searching for Chase but dancing with Craig.

The next round of songs slipped into something loud, pounding, and every person under fifty was on the dance floor moving about. Arms flailed and legs kicked, and C.J. searched the masses for any sight of Chase. Every time she caught a glimpse of him, either someone was whisking him off to dance or into a quiet corner to talk. If he wasn't the one ushered away, then she was the one escorted to the floor. Every Baron relative—and there were plenty—deemed it necessary to visit with her in motion. A few even dared to share their childhood escapades with Chase and a few more to sing his praises. She didn't need to be told what a great guy Chase Baron was. She already knew that.

After what had to be at least an hour or more of nonstop dancing, C.J. slipped away and made it halfway to the dais to sit and rest her tired feet, when Eve looped elbows and spun her about. "They're going to cut the cake now."

"Can't we watch from the table?" C.J. pointed behind her. If she ever agreed to be in another bridal party, she would ditch the trendy heels for a pair of sneakers with a solid arch support. Even combat boots if she could get away with it.

Eve shook her head. "Not if you want a good view."

All night C.J. had had a bird's-eye view of the newly married couple. Truth was, she'd had just about enough of the sappy lovebirds. Not that she wasn't happy for them—she was—but watching them became more and more painful as the evening progressed, while any hopes of connecting with Chase continued to decline.

Standing front and center of the growing crowd, C.J. spotted Chase crossing the room, his brother Craig at his side. Chase's gaze drifted from left to right and then stopped when it settled on her. One side of his mouth tipped up in the beginnings of a smile, and her muscles clenched in heated anticipation of his next move. He'd taken two, three steps, at the most, in her direction when his mother slid between him and his brother and, winding her arms in each of theirs, stopped them in place.

Disappointment doused the sparking embers and left a hollow pressure in its place. Time was running out.

"It's a beautiful wedding." Millicent Bainbridge Baron slipped in between Chase and Craig, looping her hands tightly into their elbows. To an outsider it would appear nothing more than a loving gesture between mother and sons, but Chase knew his mother was using her two eldest sons as an anchor. Attending any event with the entire Baron clan, especially one in which his father would be present, held the potential of being an emotionally shattering experience for her.

Tonight his mother had held up well. She'd smiled and laughed, and more than once Chase believed she truly had been enjoying herself. A time or two he'd spotted a shimmer in her eyes that sent chills through him or his siblings. The last thing anyone wanted was for Millicent Baron to have a meltdown at a Baron wedding. So, more than once, when he'd have preferred to cross the room to hold the woman who he had yet to proclaim his love for in his arms, he'd stayed at his mother's side instead. As had his siblings. A circle of protection.

The one saving grace was his father had had the good sense to attend sans wife number four. And bless Nancy, she'd carefully maneuvered every staged photograph to keep his parents on separate sides and yet not once did it seem out of place. She was a mastermind; no wonder Andrew called her Wonder Woman.

Chase pretended to watch the cake being cut, but, as he'd done all night, one eye shadowed C.J.'s every move. Every dance. Every smile. Every laugh. If he didn't get to hold her soon, he would very likely punch the next guy who approached her. Regardless if he was family.

Like truly civilized adults, the cake cutting and feeding went off without a hitch. Though Nancy did tease, as if she were going to shove the whole piece in Andrew's face, she instead lovingly inched a bite into his mouth. When Andrew slowly closed his lips around her finger, sucking in the small piece of cake, every woman in the room said "Aww," and every man inwardly groaned.

"I still can't believe there's a woman alive who could tame that boy." Millicent withdrew her hands from her sons and, lifting her chin, straightened her shoulders and moved forward. "I think I want to give the newest member of the family a hug."

Without looking back, Millicent strode off. Perhaps it was a sense of kindred spirits, a need to mentor an outsider on becoming a Baron. Whatever the reason, Chase thought he'd never seen his mother looking more like the woman he remembered as a young boy than right now.

"It's almost midnight," Craig said, also watching his mother's back.

"What? You turn into a pumpkin at twelve?"

Craig rolled his eyes and turned to face his brother. "This party ends at midnight, bro."

"But they just cut the cake."

"That was for show. People have been eating those little mini cupcakes since supper ended."

Chase had eaten a few himself. They were surprisingly delicious. If what Craig said was true, then Chase was running out of time. "I gotta go. Take care of Mom."

Craig bobbed his head, and Chase hurried off to the band leader.

C.J. stood rooted to the floor as Chase hurried across the floor toward the band and not to her. Had she been the fool, overplaying the importance of the little charade in her mind and her heart? The deal was done. Chase had wired the balance of the money to Bev's account yesterday before the banks closed. Spinning carefully about, C.J. made her way to the dais. She'd retrieve her small purse, go to the suite, pack, and be gone before the happy couple made their exit.

Tomorrow morning the family would gather for a final breakfast at the resort before sending off the newlyweds on a month long honeymoon at some secret destination in the South Pacific. It was the only event that C.J. hadn't been scheduled for. Early on Chase had announced she'd be returning home Sunday. Her week was over.

"I've been looking for you."

She didn't need to turn around to know Chase stood only inches behind her. His warm breath on the back of her neck sent chills scurrying down her spine.

"Dance with me?" he practically whispered.

Over her shoulder, C.J. looked into those dark blue-gray eyes. Nothing on this earth could have made her say no. Without a word she nodded.

Chase's fingers laced loosely with hers as he led them to the wooden floor. In the distance the music played a slow, easy tune. Familiarity tickled the back of her mind. Tingles traveled up her arm and spread warmly to every nerve ending. On the floor he swirled her into his arms. Not nearly as close as she would want but closer than she'd hoped for five minutes ago.

"I can't keep my eyes off of you," he sang softly.

Daring to lift her head, she listened, really listened to the song playing. "You and Me" by Lifehouse. Emotions she'd been battling were stirred with every lyric. From the ticking clock to tripping over his words to how beautiful she was. Her heart almost stopped. Air felt trapped in her lungs, and yet she continued breathing. Her feet still moving.

"I can't take my eyes off of you," he repeated as the song slowly came to an end. "It's almost midnight."

"Is it?" she whispered, barely able to find her voice.

"Our business deal will be over."

She saw so much heat in those smoky blue-gray eyes. "One week," she mumbled.

"I'd like to renegotiate."

They were still on the dance floor, but their feet had grown still.

"Something more personal."

"*Personal*?" she repeated.

"And permanent."

"*Permanent*?"

A lazy smile teased the corners of his mouth. "Why are you repeating everything I say?"

She considered answering the same as earlier in the week, but playful banter wasn't coming. "I don't want to misunderstand."

"I'm asking you to be mine. Stay with me. Please?"

"Just for tonight?"

His eyes widened slightly at the same time the bandleader called for all single women to come to the front before the last dance of the night.

Blinking slowly, he shook his head. "I'm saying this all wrong, aren't I? The Governor and Grams fell in love at first sight. Do you believe in love at first sight?"

Slowly she nodded, never taking her eyes off his. "I think I do."

"So do I." He sucked in a deep breath and blew it out slowly. "When you can answer without any doubt that you know you do, I'll have a new question for you."

Emily and Eve drew up beside them, Eve dragging a younger cousin beside her. "Come on, C.J. Time for all us single gals to duck the bouquet."

"She's not available." Chase didn't bother to look away from her. "Are you?"

C.J. faced Eve. "Sorry, but you'll have to avoid the

bouquet without me."

Emily looked terribly confused, but Eve smiled like the Cheshire cat and hurried off to the rows of women lining up center stage.

Still holding on to him, C.J. blew out a stuttered breath. "This could get complicated."

"Turns out I like complicated." Chase kissed her forehead. "I guess we do have a lot of logistics to work out."

Her eyes fluttered closed. "I'm very good at logistics. And a few other things."

"I have some talents to share too." His eyes flashed to a stormy steel color, and his grip on her tightened. "I love you, Cassandra Jane."

"I love you back, Chase Baron."

His mouth came crashing down on hers. The surrounding crowd burst into a roaring cheer. People shuffled around them. The bandleader called for all single men. And C.J. pulled away slightly, muttering against his lips, "They're calling for single men."

"A beautiful nurse already has my heart."

"And you have mine."

Across the room, Lila Baron leaned into her husband. "Our work here is done, James."

From his seat at the lead family table, the Governor lifted his gaze in the direction his wife stared. His brows creased together. "I don't know. That hard-headed boy—"

Smiling, Lila squeezed her husband's hand. "I do, dear. I do."

EPILOGUE

"All the brothers line up here." Standing in the foyer of the reception hall, the wedding coordinator waved her arms frantically at the Baron men wandering aimlessly about. Another few minutes and she had the entire wedding party and Baron family lined up for the longest receiving line Kyle had seen since the last Presidential inauguration ball.

"Smile." Eve elbowed him. "This is a happy occasion."

The wedding yes, the torturous rehearsal event, not so much. The family had endured a longwinded pastor giving excruciatingly detailed instructions on the church ceremony. Kyle and his brothers had escorted pretend guests to their seats, escorted their mom and grandmother, and then stood in line at the altar for the duration of the rehearsal. Since CJ's dad had passed away when she was a little girl, her mom was designated the one to walk her down the aisle. From the wide grin on the mom's face, the woman was delighted to be marching her daughter down the aisle. Slowly. Very slowly.

Every time they started up the long aisle of the family church, the pastor would call out to start over more slowly. At this point an injured turtle would probably make it down the aisle faster. The only two people who didn't seem at all concerned that the pastor was making them walk back and forth a bazillion times were the bride and groom. From where Kyle stood, it was obvious that if his brother's smile grew any wider his ears would disappear. The same could be said for CJ. The two kept their eyes glued to each other like a magnetic beam.

Truth was the happiness in both their faces made Kyle smile too. Perhaps not as wide, and definitely not making him as patient with the pastor as the lovebirds, but he truly was very happy for his brother. And it was even better that everyone in the family not only liked CJ, they pretty much adored her. Not to mention she had their eternal gratitude for saving Siobhan's life. And of course, for the Governor, her status as a Marine was golden. The man couldn't have hand picked a better match for his grandson if he'd tried.

"They're precious, aren't they?" Eve came up beside her brother.

"Not exactly the first word that came to mind," he shrugged, "but yeah. It's cool to see."

"You." The coordinator waved a frantic arm in Eve's direction. "Over here with the rest of the bridesmaids."

"Yes, ma'am," Eve responded like a good little soldier, and Kyle was pretty sure he heard her click her heels together before scurrying over to the other women.

He couldn't blame her. More than once he'd had the urge to salute the woman and he'd never been in the military. Thrilled when the coordinator finally announced the rehearsal was a wrap, he eagerly followed the crowd out the double doors to a smaller section of the hall that had been set up for a leisurely meal.

Immediately as the family and close friends crossed into the room, a DJ began playing music. At his side, his sister Eve began tapping her toes. Of all the Barons born to his mother and father, she seemed to be the only one who hadn't inherited two left feet. Not that he and his brothers couldn't hold their own on the dance floor. Mastering the two step and a few simple variations worked well for them. It was Eve who cut a rug worthy of a championship event.

And at the moment he was starting to wonder if Chase had been holding out on him.

While everyone settled into their seats at the table or stood at the bar ordering their libation of choice, the bride and groom had taken to the small patch of dance floor to one side of the room.

"I swear those two are going to self combust any minute." Craig handed him a cold beer. "I don't know that I've ever seen two people more in love."

Kyle held his glass up to his brother in a toast. "Amen and thank God. With this crazy family, that much love can't hurt."

"We're not that bad." Craig hefted one shoulder.

"No worse than most, but there's always something happening to keep us on our toes."

"You probably feel that way because you're the only one with a line of cars crawling up your butt at two hundred miles an hour."

Kyle shrugged. His job might be a bit riskier than either of his brothers, but ordinary people died every day slipping in the bathroom or tripping off their front porch. He was perfectly happy enjoying the thrill of living and not growing roots at a desk.

The tune playing came to an end and Chase spun his soon to be wife around and did a gentle dip. From the way CJ burst out laughing and righted herself against him, either he'd surprised her as much as the observers, or there's been a misstep he hadn't noticed. Either way, laughter was a great uniter. He'd had no doubt that these two were in it for the long haul before, but now he was even more sure that Chase and CJ were going to follow in the stable path of their grandparents and not the string of fiascos his father had called a marriage.

"So who do you think is next?" Eve came to stand by her brothers.

The two men echoed "not me" in perfect chorus.

"Well, don't look at me." Eve shook her head. "The only men who show up in my life want money or access to Mitch or the Governor."

Kyle studied his sister a moment. She was a brilliant, attractive, and kind person. Any man would be more than lucky to win her heart. But she had a point. Their family name attracted an awful lot of people with dollar signs in their eyes. His gaze shifted to Chase and CJ. Not that he was looking for a long term commitment in his life, but if he ever grew up enough to want to settle down, maybe he'd get lucky enough to find someone who looked at him the way his almost sister in law looked at his brother. Then again, maybe he should just stick to racing. Compared to making a long term relationship work, somehow his career didn't seem very risky at all.

Enjoy an excerpt from
Just One Spark

"Are you trying to give me a heart attack?" Kyle Baron's sister Eve threw her purse onto the white leather sofa on the family yacht and stood with her hands on her hips. "Do you have any idea how many years you just shaved off of my life?"

With only one hand, Kyle poured himself a drink.

Eve glared at her brother. "A little early in the day to start drinking, don't you think?"

"It would be if it were something stronger than cola." He took a slow sip of the fizzing drink. "I gather Gilbert called you?"

"He. Did."

The sharpness in his sister's voice made the hackles on the back of his neck rise. He did his best not to wince at the venomous tone. "Do I want to know what he said?"

Her hands still fisted firmly on her hips, she stared daggers at him. "I was informed, in a voice mail, that you went skydiving. That alone wasn't alarming considering speed and risk go hand and hand with you. We're all used to it. The problem is the next part. Apparently, you had a *little* accident."

He didn't dare meet her gaze.

"How the hell do you have a *little* accident falling thousands of feet out of an airplane?"

"You don't."

"Exactly." Now her foot was tapping. "I had visions of

your body splattered across miles of empty field. Piece by bloody piece."

Now he did wince.

"Thank heavens the hospital informed me you were alive before I called Mom or worse, the Governor and Grams. News like you'd been in a skydiving accident could have sent all three of them to their graves. At least all I need now is for my hairdresser to hide the newly sprouted strands of gray."

He really would have to have a chat with Gilbert about what information his manager shared with his next of kin. In Kyle's profession, there just might be a day when he really was sprawled piece by piece across a track and voice mail was not how he wanted his family told. "I'm sorry. Really."

Finally, on a long slow breath, her hands fell to her sides and a softer expression washed over her face. "Why couldn't you have been an accountant?"

That made him chuckle. His entire life his mother had tried to steer him in the direction of a stable career. What she really meant was safe. Sadly for his mother's nerves, few things in life could beat the adrenaline rush of coming across the finish line at almost 200 mph. If there was a thrill involved, whether it was on land, on the water, or in the air, Kyle was all in. To his family's chagrin, he'd opted for a high-risk land career. More precisely, racing. Precious little beat flying around a track and leaving others in your dust. The only career possibly more invigorating than racing might have been a fighter pilot. Both machines were powerful, required skilled operators with nerves of steel to maneuver, and provided the opportunity for speed on steroids. Even though there wasn't a doubt in anyone's mind that Kyle was an adrenaline junkie who had the right stuff to be a jet jock, having grown up in the limelight of a former Marine Colonel, Kyle knew following strict orders twenty-four seven was not his thing. He needed freedom and control to do what he wanted when he wanted.

Which is how he wound up here now with a very distraught sister. Still feeling the need for some of that in-flight adrenaline, skydiving was his ticket. What he hadn't expected was for the statistics on his way of life to kick in now. Too many drivers fell into adversity not on the track as spectators would expect, but after the races. As with drivers who survived long careers behind the wheel unscathed only to be taken out skiing or cleaning gutters, he'd enjoyed an injury free career so far only to find himself in a cast for the next six weeks, not from a racetrack mishap, not even from his recent tumble out of an airplane. No, his broken wrist came from slipping on a bar of soap while changing in the men's room after successfully skydiving on a clear sunny day.

"How long are you out for?"

Lost in his own thoughts about the stupid fall, the extra challenges his absence from the circuit would mean for his team and the green back up driver, he struggled for the words to make his sister feel at least a little better. "Maybe six weeks."

"Maybe?" One brow rose higher than the other, and shaking her head, she blew out a sigh and stood up. "I think I need that drink."

"Isn't it a little early in the day," he teased.

"It's five o'clock somewhere."

Kyle followed his sister to the bar and too quickly realized with only one working hand, he was not going to be uncorking wine bottles anytime soon. At least the injury had happened during the summer break—one of the reason's he'd gone skydiving at all. With three weeks left to the natural hiatus, he'd only miss one or two season races at best.

"So." She poured half a glass of her favorite white merlot. "What's the plan?"

"Plan?"

"Yes. You're injured. Last time I looked, even if you could work the paddle shifters, there's no way to undo your harness and remove the steering wheel fast enough to qualify for the race with one hand in a cast."

Didn't he know that one. It also didn't help any that the darn wrist was throbbing despite the meds the doctor had given him. "No driving for now."

"And jumping out of airplanes? Or do you need two hands for that?"

"One hand will do, but I'm not planning on going back out anytime soon."

"Well, there's that." She took a slow sip of her wine. "At least none of us will have to worry for a little while."

And that darn near broke his heart. As much as he loved racing for a living, he hated worrying his family. "I really am sorry Gilbert scared you."

"I know." For the first time since she'd stomped onto the yacht, the corners of her mouth tipped upward in a tired smile. She leaned in and kissed his cheek. "I have an idea."

"Should I be worried?" Sometimes his brilliant geeky sister came up with fantastic ideas, and other times, well, he and his brothers were better off running for the hills.

She rolled her eyes skyward. "Since you can't try and kill yourself for the next few weeks, why don't you recuperate at the ranch? Grams would love to have you and I think having you intact under her roof will make this little accident more palatable."

His kid sister had a point. At least this idea wouldn't be so awful. As a matter of fact, it was a pretty good idea. He loved the ranch as much as the yacht, but moored off shore, the Baroness could start to feel stifling, especially for six weeks. Yep, bless his little sister, she was right, the ranch and his grandmother's love was just what the doctor ordered.

Addison Raymond stared at the screen in front of her, shook her head, and then picking up a traditional number two pencil, began scribbling on a scratch pad.

"I don't know how you use those things." Her coworker Jen stood in the entryway of the oversized cubicle that didn't quite qualify as a private office.

"You know I don't like mechanical pencils." Even as a little kid, she loved drawing with sharpened pencils. To her, mechanical pencils always felt dull. There was also something soothing about the whirring sound of an electric pencil sharpener.

"You also may be the only person in the building who actually sharpens pencils."

"That's not possible." There were plenty of old fogies in her department who still used pencils, adding machines, and white board. Though in all honesty, she had no idea why those same people had a deep rooted aversion to software. Still struggling with her latest project, she tossed the pencil down, leaned back in the chair and smiled up at her friend. "Can I help with anything?"

Jen shook her head. "Not unless you know someone looking for a mechanical engineer who hasn't done engineering in a very long while."

"What? Why?"

"Deb in personnel just told me on the QT that an emergency board meeting was called this morning."

Addison glanced down the hall. She couldn't see the executive board room from her space, but she had noticed the CEO and a few other company bigwigs getting off the elevator a couple of hours ago. "Are we sure it's not a scheduled meeting? You know how the good old boys love an excuse to show off to each other."

"I wish. Rumor is that the quarterly reports are in and are disastrous. Next quarter's forecast isn't any better."

"This won't be the first time the numbers have been bad. We've weathered economic downturns before and survived."

Jen spun around and leaned back on the desk. "This time feels different. Electric cars and green energy weren't as popular as they are now."

"Or as politically correct." As much as she wished it weren't so, there was a knot in her stomach that had been twisting every so often with the negative news reports and industry gossip. "Let's just hope the grapevine has got it all wrong."

"I hope so."

As difficult as it was, Addison did her best to paste on a reassuring smile. "Like I said, we've weathered worse."

"From your mouth to God's ears." Jen pushed away from the desk. "I'd better get back to my cubby. Just in case you're right and I really do still have a job."

"There you go," Addison chuckled, "positive attitude."

Jen rolled her eyes and raising one finger in the air in an off handed wave, continued down the hall.

Reaching for her freshly sharpened pencil, Addison returned to the challenges at hand. She knew the answer was right in front of her and she simply wasn't seeing it. Maybe it was time for a little fresh air. Clean her mental pallet. Between her cubicle here in town and her office at home, she spent too much time hovered over a desk. She really did need to stop taking her work home with her. Spend more down time with friends. Catch a movie in a real theater with real surround sound. She didn't dare stop to reflect on how long had it been since she'd spent an hour with anyone who wasn't on the company payroll.

As soon as this project was finalized, she'd do that. She would, but for now, water bottle in hand, she strolled down the hall and pushed the elevator button. One of the things she loved about working in downtown Houston this time of year was access to the rooftop patio. A few minutes high above the world might give her new perspective.

The door behind her opened and one by one, the company executives filed out of the board room. Low murmurs filled the narrow hallway slowly ebbing to unnatural silence. The elevator door opened and she was tempted to lag behind in case anyone actually said anything important, hopefully reassuring. Instead, she went about her business. After all, that's what she was getting paid for, not for eavesdropping.

Three of the dozen execs stepped into the elevator with her. The silence hung heavily. Using the special key for the senior executive floor, the three others exited the small space in continued silence. The ropes that had twisted on and off in her stomach recently, now weighed heavily inside her. Like it or not, her gut screamed Jen was right. Something very unpleasant just went down in that all-morning meeting and if in the end she wasn't looking for a new job, then her name wasn't Addison Lynn Raymond.

Read more of Just One Spark available now

MEET CHRIS

Author of dozens of contemporary novels, including the award winning Aloha Series, Chris Keniston lives in suburban Dallas with her husband, two human children, and two canine children. Though she loves her puppies equally, she admits being especially attached to her German Shepherd rescue. After all, even dogs deserve a happily ever after.

More on Chris and her books can be found at www.chris keniston.com.

Follow Chris on facebook at ChrisKenistonAuthor or on twitter @ckenistonauthor.

Join Chris' newsletter! Enjoy inside peeks and photographs from Chris' world and stories. Some times she'll thank her subscribers with a free copy of a new 99 cent flirt.

Please, if you enjoyed reading Just One Date, consider helping other readers find The Billionaire Barons of Texas Series by taking a moment to leave a review. Reviews are a blessing to authors and readers alike. Even just a few words will do! Thank you.

9 781942 561798